THE LAST ASHOKA

THE LAST ASHOKA

VIVEK PAI

ADHYYAN BOOKS

© **Vivek Pai**

The Last Ashoka

1st Edition

All rights reserved

Publication Date: August 2018

Price: ₹ 396 | $ 14.99

ISBN: 978-93-87502-49-9

Published by:

Adhyyan Books

Office No. 637,

Opposite Vivanta by Taj,

DDA SFS. Pocket-1, Dwarka,

Sec-22, New Delhi-110077

Website: www.adhyyanbooks.com

E-mail: contact@adhyyanbooks.com

Acknowledgments

To my

Gurus and Teachers

Mother and Late Father

Wife, Aarati

Son, Varad and Daughter, Saanika

Family and Friends

Beagle, Snoopy

For Valuable Contribution and Editing Inputs Special Thanks

To

Ritu Goyal Harish

Harinath Pabbathi

Introduction

Bhaarata is the popular name by which the land now called India is known to the natives. This word *Bhaarata* has its roots in the Sanskrit language and it means, 'To be in harmony with Nature.'

This land has been the home of many great *Seers* and *Sages* who were responsible for disseminating great knowledge and wisdom to the entire humanity.

These wise souls understood the cyclic phenomena of nature. They called a time cycle, an epoch or an era, of 4.32 million solar years as *Maha Yuga*. This cyclical epoch is divided into four parts – The *Satya Yuga* or the Age of the Truth which lasts for 1,728,000 years; *Treta Yuga* in which virtues start diminishing slowly and lasts for 1,296,000 years; *Dwapara Yuga* during which diseases and discontent become rampant and lasts for 864,000 years; and *Kali Yuga*, which is the present age of ignorance and lasts for 432,000 years.

The laboratories they worked in were the great depths of their minds, and their teacher was Mother Nature. The knowledge and wisdom these Masters generated and passed on to their pupils were coded as various Sciences which have stood the scrutiny of time.

However, there were ignorant people from outside *Bhaarata* who copied this knowledge in the previous millennium to create their own counterfeit versions that were not in synchronisation with the Universal laws of nature.

The wisdom of this land, however, was out of the league with those immature minds and has largely remained untouched and could not be adulterated.

Every inch of this land is soaked with the wisdom of the masters of the past. However, it has also been soaked with the blood of innocents due to the ignorance and arrogance of the physically mightier people.

This work of fiction is an attempt to pay tribute to some of those great souls of the past. It is also an attempt to explore how some of these people from the past can shape the future of this great land *Bhaarata*, and eventually change the course of humanity.

This is also an endeavour to unfold some aspects of 'Eternal Way of Life' of the people of this land known as *Sanathana Dharma* by the inhabitants of this ancient land *Bhaarata*.

Before the Epilogue

The 72-year-old potter enters the river Ganga for his early morning bath and prayers. His oval face has lines drawn deep by time on his shining rubbery skin. His head is bald except for a short mane of silvery white hair with streaks of black that are tied into a knot. Age has presented a slight stoop to his six-foot body which is slender due to his daily practice of *Yogasanas*. Even though he is 72 years in age, he does not look that old.

He folds his hands in the direction of the Sun and takes a dip in the cool water. His wet saffron dress now looks crimson with the first rays of the daylight as he rises. With both his palms facing the sky, he dips his hands in this life-giving river and prays for the welfare of this great land.

To a stranger, he would have looked like one of the thousands of *Yogis* visiting this holy city. He was certainly a *Yogi* – a *Karma Yogi* comparable to the one who inhabited this land many millennia earlier. Ashoka had shown by his actions that he was truly a great *Karma Yogi*.

While slowly coming out of the Ganga, he hears the splash created by the collision of the holy water against the sacred land. Somewhere in the background, he can faintly hear the melodious music of the stringed instrument *Surbahar,* accompanied by the rhythmic beats of the *Pakhawaj.*

He walks along the narrow by-lanes of this world's oldest and invariably inhabited city of Kashi. As passersby greet him, he nods with a smile and greets them with folded hands. Everyone seems to know him as he is their beloved guide who had shaped the destiny of this country. He is as comfortable in the midst of people, as he was on his potter's wheel shaping clay to create articles of daily use.

This day marks his return to pottery, the family profession, after 63 eventful years.

He was born in a *Kumhar* or potter's family, at Chunar. His parents had named him Ashoka as they were greatly inspired by the great Mauryan Emperor under whose patronage the potters had seen a golden era more than two millennia earlier. He carried the family surname *Prajapati.*

He could feel droplets of rain fall on him. This was an auspicious sign from the heavens. He looked at the sky and folded his hands in gratitude.

He now had to travel another 30 kilometres to reach his ancestral home at Chunar.

Under his leadership, this land which he was born in was now fully rid of centuries of barbarian influence.

Centuries earlier, various barbarians who were in their dark ages had entered this land repeatedly from the North and West to plunder the material riches about which they had heard of in their far-off lands.

They were successful in pitting brother against brother, neighbour against neighbour and friend against friend. All riches visible to those crude brains were taken away. They even stole the vast treasures of written knowledge that included various sciences, and this partly helped those barbarians come out of their ignorant ways.

However, the real treasure, the wisdom of multiple millennia, could not be seen or understood by these people and was left behind. This wisdom was imprinted in every grain of sand, every drop of water, every molecule of air and thus formed a part of the very DNA of every living being born in this land.

The wisdom of this land and its people would show humans elsewhere on this planet how to live – and how to live a great life– in synchrony with nature, while also being visibly rich.

This return of the golden age was even greater than the previous ones.

The events from 20 years earlier in 2056 CE, coupled with the history of past 1500 years had made the people of this land cautious. To ensure that these chapters of history do not repeat ever again, major changes were made.

It was also enshrined in the Constitution that – "Aggressors, barbarians, looters and plunderers alongside their supporters will be treated as barbarians. They will be dealt with all the power and might available to the people of this land with the swiftness in the most barbaric way possible."

Pakistan - 2056 CE

General Rizwan Pasha put on his cap as he got out of the military vehicle. He looked at his new uniform. It still had a smell of freshness that was now mixed with the fragrance of Rose *Attar*. He then adjusted the medals hanging on his chest. His shoes were spotless and shining. He thought, "Everything has to be perfect today."

Today was the last Friday of this Holy month of Ramadan. He had arrived directly at the Military Command Centre after his morning prayers.

A drop of rain fell on his shoes and made him look upwards. The sky was dark and overcast. The wind had come to a standstill, and it looked like it would pour heavily.

He thought, "It is unusual. It never rains at this time of the year."

Suddenly an approaching buzzing sound distracted his attention. It was originating from a swarm of insects closing in towards him. As the swarm swooshed over him, he thought he heard the word 'Coward'.

General Rizwan Pasha was called the 'Coward of Pakistan' and he had never made any effort to change this. In fact, he had made every effort not to change this. He was playing his pawns carefully one by one and being addressed as the 'Coward of Pakistan' was a part of his master plan.

It was fine with him when humans called him that but Rizwan was shocked that these insects were calling him a 'coward'. He shrugged as he entered Military Command Centre. Maybe it was his imagination he thought. From the corner of his eyes he saw a few of those wasps like insects fly in after him.

He did not want any distractions today. The dark clouds and this swarm of insects had both given him just that. They were not a part of his master plan, which was now in the last stage of execution. He knew he was helpless and had no control over these aspects of nature.

He entered the large room that had 200 people and proceeded to sit at the head of the large horse-shoe shaped table in the centre. His entire chain of top commanders was on either side of this table. They sat on his instruction. The others in the room sat after them.

The atmosphere in this Command Centre was now electric. All 200 pairs of eyes were looking in his direction for his instructions.

He looked around and confirmed that all the last pieces were now in place.

A smile escaped his thin lips and this helped ease the atmosphere a bit.

No words or emotions could probably describe the elation he was experiencing now.

Henceforth, the enemy would always feel that the raiders and plunderers of the past including Ghori, Ghazni, Timur and Babur were very kind compared to what was to happen today.

A twisted grin escaped him as he thought, "Today is the day of retribution. Today is the day of revenge. Today is the day of total destruction and annihilation. This is Judgment Day."

Young Potter

Ashoka was born at Chunar in 2004 CE.

Chunar is an ancient town known for its immense natural beauty, exotic waterfalls, historical significance and religious places of worship.

One legend says that Lord Vishnu appeared in *Satya Yuga* as Vamana or a dwarf and begged to the generous King Bali for three feet of land. Bali readily agreed to give what was asked of him. It was then, Lord Vishnu assumed a gigantic form – Trivikrama – and covered all areas that Bali ruled over with just two steps. His first step was on the hills in Chunar, and He left his footmark there. This place came to be known as Charanadri or Chunar the shortened version.

Chunar is also well-known for its clay pottery industry ever since the Mauryan period. About 10,000 potters are engaged in this craft.

Pottery has great significance in the *Sanathana Dharma*. 'Kumbha' and 'Kalasha' are the vessels which are said to mirror the shape of the primordial cosmic universe and are used in all rituals and ceremonies beginning with birth, then marriage and eventually death. These vessels serve as a reminder of this understanding, as well as the knowledge of the cyclic nature of all matter.

The vessel making tradition goes back in time and history to the primordial *Kalasha* or pot. This pot is said to have carried the *Amrut* or the 'Divine Nectar of Immortality' obtained after the churning of the celestial ocean and this *Amrut* is said to have given immortality to the Gods.

The potters or *Prajapati*s of Chunar have many such legends, which are transmitted from generation to generation by stories or by ballads.

Radheshyam was one such *Prajapati* and came from a lineage of traditional potters. His wife, Nirmala Devi, and he had nine children. Their youngest son was named Ashoka in fond remembrance of the third Mauryan Emperor.

Being the youngest ensured that Ashoka was the beloved of the house. Learning came quite easily to this boy. He found formal schooling very boring and was easily distracted from the open air classes he used to attend. He had a very inquisitive approach and used to love learning from observing nature.

Ashoka had learnt pottery at an early age following the tradition of a *Prajapati Kumbhar*. This included the art of identifying the right clay, mixing ingredients in the right proportions, making pots and other pottery, drying it and baking it and finally decorating the finished products.

Today was a hectic day and the whole family was busy. Suddenly, Radheshyam noticed that Ashoka was the only one missing. He called out loudly, "Where is Ashoka?"

His wife replied from inside the house. "He must be at his usual place."

Ram and Shyam, the elder sons looked at each other and smiled, as they knew what was to come next. Just then Radheshyam came and indicted to them. They had to go and get Ashoka back home as usual. They knew he would be swimming in the river Ganga near the Chunar Fort.

The Chunar fort is on an extension of the Vindhya mountain range and was built initially by King Vikramaditya of Ujjain as a home for his brother Raja Bharthari, who had become a *Sadhu*.

Ram and Shyam reached the river and literally dragged Ashoka out of the river.

On their way back home Ashoka said he was tired and sat on one of the large golden coloured cylindrical sandstone blocks. Ashoka did not know why, but sitting here always helped him relax. Ram and Shyam sat after him and started looking around at the large blocks of unfinished stone carvings.

This was the same quarry that had been used 2300 years earlier by the artisans of the Emperor Ashokavadhana Maurya. The Ashoka pillars and edicts made of hard fine-grained sandstone and erected throughout the Mauryan Empire were quarried here.

As the three of them reached near their house, Ashoka called out to their neighbour Ramu kaka and asked him to repeat his favourite story. Ram and Shyam stood next to him as Ramu kaka started narrating this legend for a zillionth time - "At the time of creation, Lord Brahma, the Creator created *Prajapatis*, or the potters, and assigned them the task of making pots. The other two Gods of this trinity shared their weapons with these *Prajapatis*. Lord Vishnu, the Preserver gave his *Sudarshan Chakra* or Disc to them to serve as their wheel, Lord Shiva, the Destroyer gave his *Trishul* or Trident to turn the wheel. Lord Brahma finally gave a string from his sacred thread by which a finished pot could be detached from the wheel.

Prajapati is, hence considered the male who operates the wheel and creates. The Earth is considered the female, the matter that we *Prajapatis* use to create."

They then quietly slid into their backyard where all the remaining brothers were working on the red clay got from river Ganga. They were making statues, lamps, decorative pieces, toys. The parents and sisters were working in the front yard with the white clay got from the ponds and lakes. Ashoka knew they would be preparing ceramic products including toys, cups, plates, jars and dinner sets.

Ashoka sat in front of his father's wheel. What fascinated this young potter most was working on his wheel while making pottery. The way this simple wheel was spun around with a stick, the quick movement of pushing with his hands, the pouring of the water over the cone of clay placed in the middle of the wheel and pulling it up, the wheel momentum that helped him to create a circular pot, the ability to slowly shape the clay with his hands and then separating it from the clay cone with a thread, and lifting it delicately and keeping it in a place to dry; all of this seemed as great mysteries to him. This simple creative act would create rounded clay pitchers and pots that would later be used by people.

Ashoka was nine years old now and was working tirelessly on the wheel to create pots. The entire family would shortly leave for Prayag to be a part of the *Maha Kumbha Mela*.

Maha Kumbha Mela – Prayag 2014 CE

Prayag is amongst the oldest known cities of this Earth and has been a silent witness to almost every episode of human history. It is a city located at the *Sangam,* which is the union of Ganga, Yamuna and Saraswati (invisible now), the three sacred rivers.

Kumbha Mela is one of the largest religious gatherings in the world. *Mela* is a gathering or a fair. *Kumbha* refers to the constellation Aquarius. There are many other interpretations or stories related to the use of this word.

Kumbha Mela takes place at four places - Prayag, Haridwar, Ujjain and Nashik. At each of these locations, the *Purna,* which means total or full, *Kumbha Mela* is held once in 12 years.

There is a time difference of around 3 years between the *Kumbha Melas* at Haridwar and Prayag. However, the *Melas* at Nashik and Ujjain are celebrated in the same year or one year apart.

The exact date is determined according to the Luni-Solar *Vikram Samvat* calendar coupled with a combination of zodiac positions, the position of the Sun, the Jupiter and the Moon.

The twelfth *Purna Kumbha Mela* is called the *Maha Kumbha Mela* and occurs at each of these locations once every 144 years.

In addition to the sheer magnitude of *Kumbha Mela*, the enthusiasm, energy, different sounds and the multitude of colours make this festival unique.

The rivers at each of these places are central to this *Mela*. The belief of having a bath in these rivers on auspicious occasions is what brings most people here.

Some are here to entertain, while some others come to enjoy the show. There are a few who come to spend their last days on earth in this holy place before dying. Then, there are people who are here to cater to the needs and wants of this huge gathering. Yet there is a category of people who come in search of the 'meaning of life' and to understand the 'deeper mysteries of existence.'

Great Masters or *Gurus* come here to ensure that their physical presence will guide some souls in the right direction.

Gurudev was one such Great Master. *Gurudev* literally meant that he is a *Dev* (God) of the *Gurus* (Masters). That was the only name that was used to address him.

His bulky body was about 5' 8" in height. He had small round greyish-black eyes with a bright wrinkled face surrounding them. His round face perfectly matched the shape of his large pot-belly. He wore only a piece of saffron cloth around his waist which covered his thighs. His white hair had almost fused with each other due to lack of care and it covered all of his large broad back. His age was something that made people considered in awe - he is said to have been living for 108 years as on this *Maha Kumbha Mela*. Even more mind-boggling was the fact that he had taken up two additional bodies one after another. He is supposed to have done this after each of his two earlier bodies had to be cast off.

Most of *Gurudev*'s time was spent in the Himalayas, and he would visit one of the *Kumbha Mela* every few years. This was the time for some of his pupils to come back from their Himalayan retreat and integrate with the society. It was also the time when he took new disciples on his return to the Himalayas. Many of his other followers would take this opportunity to spend time in his presence and also take his guidance. Many *Sadhus* also would look forward to having his *Darshan* (being in his presence). In his company, one could get a calm and serene feeling as though time had come to a standstill.

Radheshyam and his family, like other *Prajapati* potters, would come to the *Kumbha Mela* for a variety of reasons. It was a market for their pottery besides being a pleasant diversion from their routine life at Chunar.

They would start early to reach there a few weeks before the *Kumbha Mela* festivities started and set up makeshift roadside shops. These shops would be manned by different family members, taking turns. This ensured that other members would enjoy the festive atmosphere trying different things to eat, buying colourful clothes and getting entertained from all the street shows and ceremonies. The older members of the family would look forward to visiting different holy places and meeting *sadhus*.

Radheshyam remembered his great-grandfather, grandfather and his father telling him about Gurudev when he was as old as his youngest son Ashoka.

He also remembered his last meeting with Gurudev in 2004 at the Ujjain *Kumbha Mela*. Gurudev had told Radheshyam, "The next time we meet, you will have something to offer to me."

Ever since that time till today he had never understood what Gurudev had meant. He knew he would find out soon during this visit.

Radheshyam, along with most of the members of the large family, entered Gurudev's tent. There were about 30 people already in this large enclosure set up by the government in a designated area for the *Sadhus*. Radheshyam patiently waited for Gurudev to speak to him.

Finally, when most of the visitors had left, Gurudev summoned Radheshyam and Nirmala Devi to him.

After Gurudev blessed the couple, he addressed them, "You are aware of the different *Yugas* (Ages) and their cyclic nature. The time had come to make the preparations before the present *Kali Yuga* ends and get humans ready for the new *Satya Yuga*."

He looked at Radheshyam and told him that he and his wife also had a role in that. He reminded them of the offering they had to make. Gurudev then looked in Ashoka's direction and told the couple, "This nine-year-old boy has to play a key role in shaping humanity as he had done in his past life." He then added, "The time has come for Ashoka to be prepared for his role, and he will have to accompany me to *Padma Dham* in the Himalayas."

Radheshyam and Nirmala Devi could not believe what they had just heard. They looked at each other and immediately fell at Gurudev's feet for having chosen Ashoka. It was the first time that a member of the *Prajapati* community had been chosen to follow Gurudev's footsteps. It was indeed a great honour and blessing. Gurudev blessed the couple and then summoned Ashoka to his side.

After Gurudev had blessed the boy, he pointed to a tall 18-year-old wearing a white dress and said "This is Acharya. He has been with me since the last *Kumbha Mela* and it is now time for him to move on into the world."

Ashoka would take Acharya's place in *Padma Dham*.

Chanakya

Vishnu was born in a financially backward family in Pushkar. He was the second child and had three siblings. His father had a small shop which catered to repairs of all kinds of electronic goods. He helped his father at the shop and quickly mastered his father's trade at an early age.

His interests in sciences meant that he would learn more of electronics. During his graduation in Electronics, he developed a fascination for Aeronautics. He eventually completed his post-graduation in Aeronautics from the Indian Institute of Science (IISc).

He was recruited by a US company and started working in America in their research department. Robotics was becoming popular and his educational background eventually drew him closer to the subject. Within two years, he had saved enough money and joined Cal Tech Institute for his doctorate in Robotics.

Post the doctoral studies, he was picked up by one of the top corporate in Robotics. However, within a year, he was disillusioned with the work culture of viewing everything in terms of quick profits that would eventually pay fat dividends to the already rich.

From an early age, he had been deeply influenced by Kautilya, more popularly known as Chanakya. Kautilya was a great teacher who had shaped the history of this country about 2400 years ago.

Vishnu changed his name to Chanakya. This new Chanakya had made up his mind and took a pledge - "I despise the thought of being a resource for the rich or being a part of the well-oiled global financial machinery. I will live an honourable life rather than help the rich become richer. I would rather spread the knowledge I have to help those who don't have the means to learn. I will dedicate myself to educating and uplifting the lives of the underprivileged."

He returned to India and spent the next 3 years travelling all over the country trying to understand the needs of financially marginalised people.

During his travel, he found that the education imparted to the poor sections of the society was substandard and mediocre at best. He consequently started developing a network of teachers who were keen to change this.

He also saw that many of the beggars in the country were young children. They were driven to begging by their parents and the begging mafia, which saw these as a means to make a financial fortune using these innocent lives. Chanakya understood that these kids were extremely resourceful. He started slowly developing a network which would connect these kids to him. Eventually, step by step, he wanted them to be independent and out of the clutches of their exploiters.

The thirty-year-old Chanakya had now reached Prayag for the largest gathering of mankind in 2014 – The *Maha Kumbha Mela*. He was sure that this gathering would help him develop his network further.

Within nine days of his stay at Prayag, the kids who now formed his network suggested that he should visit a great sadhu Gurudev for darshan.

This meeting with Gurudev would eventually be a life-defining moment for him. This meeting would not only help him in his cause but also help him make a significant contribution to the way humans would eventually shape up.

Chanakya entered the tent and saw Gurudev seated on a dais. There were many people standing beside him. There were about three dozen people sitting in front of Gurudev waiting for their turn to be blessed by him. Chanakya went and sat among these people. As he waited for his turn, he saw that there were many other sadhus who had come to pay their respect to Gurudev. This clearly meant that Gurudev was revered even by those who were themselves respected and had their own following.

About 30 minutes after he had entered the tent, Gurudev pointed his finger at Chanakya and beckoned with his fingers to come on the dais. Chanakya approached him and was about to speak when Gurudev kept his forefinger on his lips suggesting that he should not to say anything. Then Gurudev started speaking.

What he heard from Gurudev stunned him! Gurudev had given him a quick story of his past and it was as though Gurudev knew everything of Chanakya's past. For a person of science and reasoning, Chanakya quickly tried to find a logical explanation for Gurudev knowing details about his life.

Gurudev, as if reading his thoughts told him, "Don't be concerned about how I know about your past, instead concentrate on what you want to do further in life and how you will do it."

Chanakya now understood that Gurudev also knew what he was supposed to do. Gurudev had reminded him of events from his past, just to impress upon him to follow what was to be said next.

Gurudev pointed to Acharya and said, "Time has come for both Acharya and you to travel together to Ujjain and start your work from there."

Next, he pointed his fingers at a group of people sitting and informed: "These people will guide you both to your destination."

Journey to Padma *Dham*

After the *Maha Kumbha Mela* ended, Gurudev and Ashoka started on their journey to *Padma Dham* in the Himalayas. Gurudev had informed him that they would take the ancient route by walking along the banks of the river Ganga most of the time. However, they would take a shorter route in places where the river was too winding significantly prolonging their journey.

They would stop at various *Ashrams* (monasteries of *sadhus*) all along the way. Many of these *sadhus* were disciples of Gurudev. However, others were masters of a different tradition of other *Gurus*. They would generally rest overnight at these places and proceed after sunrise.

On their way, Gurudev had started teaching Ashoka the basics of Sanskrit. He taught how the word 'Sanskrit' was derived from the union of the prefix 'Sam' of the word 'Samyak' which meant 'total' and 'krit' that indicates 'done.' Thus, he taught, "The word 'Sanskrit' means that this language is perfect or complete in terms of communication

- whether for - reading or, hearing, and also for the use of its vocabulary to transcend and express an emotion."

He went on to explain how Sanskrit is rich in its vocabulary, phonology, grammar, and syntax, which remains undiluted in its purity to this day. He then gave further details of 52 letters used, its 16 vowels and the 36 consonants.

Gurudev explained, "When you add rules and grammar to Sanskrit words, it becomes a structured language. You can compare it with the skeleton that gives a structure to the human body. This is very necessary for a better understanding and to clearly convey the various sciences and knowledge we know. There are times when this structure creates a hindrance, like in the case of learning of the age-old wisdom. Thus, while learning the Vedas, many of these rules are not used. Thus, we get more moods and help this language move freely like a snake that can slide into the smallest of holes."

Ashoka had learnt Sanskrit at school. However, he noticed that there was a significant difference in the way his teachers at Chunar had taught him. Gurudev's method was ancient and was so subtle in its teaching that he could instantly get a total grasp of what was taught.

They stopped at the ashram of Gargi Maa during this journey. She was a 70-year-old *Sadhvi* (holy woman) who was a learned wise person with a great knowledge of the ancient scriptures. Gurudev directed her to teach Ashoka forms of ancient logic which would be further helpful for his learning at *Padma Dham*.

She educated Ashoka on *Nyaya,* the ancient science of logic and discernment one has to use to identify valid sources of knowledge. She explained, "It is very important to acquire the right knowledge and learn to distinguish these from false opinions."

"There are four *Pramanas* or proofs or methods of identifying this right knowledge. These four are perception, inference, comparison and evidence. The information obtained through each of these could still be either valid or invalid. Hence, it is necessary to further process this information by creating a variety of explanatory methods and analysis."

Even though she had not expected Ashoka to understand fully what was being taught, she had done so as Gurudev had told her. She was surprised by the ability with which the lad quickly grasped and easily understood whatever she had taught. However, Gargi Maa cautioned Ashoka to regularly practice *Nyaya* and learn much more to sharpen his logic.

After 21 days of stay with Gargi Maa, Gurudev and Ashoka continued on to *Padma Dham*.

On the way, Gurudev had also started teaching *Yoga* to Ashoka. He explained how this ancient science referred to the union of an individual soul to the Infinite. It was necessary for a student to prepare the body first, proceed to prepare the mind and eventually, this would lead to *Kaivalya* or the reunion with the Infinite.

Gurudev then described the eight limbs of *Yoga* or components which led a seeker to the ultimate goal, step by step.

"First are the *Yamas* or the moral rules by which a student has to live. The behaviours that have to be inculcated or *Niyamas* come next. Third are the *Asanas* or body postures one has to practice for disciplining the body. *Pranayama* came next and is the regulation of breath. Mastery over breath led to mastery over thoughts." explained Gurudev.

Once Ashoka had developed proficiency in these four, he could next proceed to *Pratyahara* which meant that he could now consciously try to move away from sensory perceptions.

"*Dharana* and *Dhyana* are the sixth and seventh limbs which refer to single-pointed focus of the mind and to practice non-judgmental contemplation."

Finally, Gurudev described *Samadhi* in which a soul attains oneness or union with the Infinite using various types of meditation practices, which would be individually decided by every Guru based on the pupil's specific nature.

Gurudev and Ashoka had now travelled most of the distance to *Padma Dham* and had reached the Valley of Flowers.

Before arriving here, Gurudev had taught Ashoka how to regulate his breath while travelling through some parts of this Valley of Flowers which would be in full bloom at this time. This was in addition to the roots they consumed that would also help them cross this area and the adjoining forest without any adverse effects. "These roots are equally necessary to avoid the hallucinogenic effects of some aromatic flower varieties that will be in full bloom now," said Gurudev.

Once they had crossed the valley of flowers, they started travelling through the forest and halted for the night at the hut of Aghori Baba, who was another of Gurudev's disciples.

Aghori Baba was about 80 years old. His skin sagged in some parts and in others showed most outlines of the bones of the body. His dark black eyes seemed to be popping out of their sockets. He lived alone and never spoke much to anyone. Gurudev had informed Ashoka that they communicated by transmitting thoughts to each other.

This would be their last halt before reaching *Padma Dham*.

Padma Dham

The next day, after walking for about three hours, Gurudev faced a small grove of bamboos and started walking towards it. The grove seemed to be resting against a large rock that was behind it. Once they reached the grove Gurudev separated two bamboo tree-shoots that had thrown all their weight on each other. A crevice in the rock behind revealed itself. Gurudev slid through this crevice and gestured to Ashoka to follow him. Ashoka understood that this crevice led them to their destination as they now started to climb their way to the top of one of the mountains.

After a while, they reached a flatter area on the mountain which was not the peak but somewhere midway to the peak. It was foggy, and nothing below or above was visible. Gurudev faced the north and moved both his hands sideways as if waving the fog away. All of a sudden, the fog vanished and the valley below showed itself very clearly with the light of the sun which was now right above their head.

The valley looked like a perfect circle which reminded Ashoka of the number zero. In the centre was a massive tree which looked like a *banyan* tree with its roots hanging from its branches. Facing them in the north was a waterfall dropping crystal clear glacial water. The water collecting at the bottom of the fall seemed to split into two and flowed along two channels from one end of the valley to another and formed sides of what seemed to be an equilateral triangle. Two small circular water bodies were at the other two corners of this triangle connected by a third channel. The water body on the east looked calm and crystal clear. The one on the west had the water bubbling with a lot of steam coming out resembling an open geyser. Gurudev informed Ashoka that all the glacial water from the waterfall eventually disappeared due to this hot geyser. Ashoka could spot five large trees which formed a perfect circle around the *Banyan* tree. They were *Peepal, Bael, Neem, Chandan,* and *Chaityavriksha,* said Gurudev. Eight smaller hills formed the perimeter of this valley. Ashoka counted twelve larger snow capped mountains surrounding these hills. Gurudev corrected him saying that the number was, in fact, thirteen. Ashoka realised that he had missed the mountain they stood on.

This entire sight was mesmerising. Nothing Ashoka had seen till now could be compared to the gripping beauty of this place. If there was a Heaven, then here it was. All the colourful plants coupled with their aroma in this valley truly made it hypnotic.

Suddenly a thought crossed Ashoka's mind. He asked Gurudev, "The Mountains and the hills surrounding this valley look like the petals of a flower. Is this the reason for its name - *Padma Dham*?"

Gurudev said that at the physical level he was right. He added, "*Padma* or the Lotus is a flower that represents the ultimate flowering. *Dham* is a place where the attachments created by the body are washed off. The union of the *Atma*, an Individual Soul, with the *Paramatma* or the Infinite Soul is considered the ultimate flowering of a human body. Since time immemorial, this place has been the abode of many *Atmas* who have approached their final journey. They have been guided and prepared for this concluding passage by the great sages at this place. So, *Padma Dham* is a place where the ultimate flowering of all those souls has taken place and will continue to do so."

When they finally reached the valley, Ashoka saw many cave openings in the hills and mountains. There were also many plants, flowers and fruits that he was witnessing for the first time.

As they approached the banyan tree in the centre, he saw that some hanging roots had come on to the ground and formed a seating arrangement. Gurudev took his seat here. Many of the disciples came and paid their respect to Gurudev.

Ashoka sat on the ground in front of Gurudev looking around him in wonder.

This would be the place where Ashoka would spend time learning and meditate for the next few years.

Acharya's Journey

Soon after Gurudev's *Kumbha Mela* proclamation to Acharya to move into the world, he along with Chanakya had left with a bow to the master.

Just as Acharya was going out of the tent, he saw some little kids playing. He put his hand into his saffron shoulder bag, pulled out some apples and gave them to the kids. The bag was lighter now with just his extra pair of clothes. The seeds of the fruits he had eaten earlier were in a small pouch stitched into this bag. Chanakya smiled as he passed these kids and waved at them as if to say goodbye.

"I am 20 years old now and have spent the last 10 years with Gurudev at *Padma Dham*. In 2004, I was just a boy of 10 years and came with my parents and relatives for Ujjain *Kumbha Mela*," Acharya informed Chanakya.

Acharya had lost all his family members in a boat accident. He had managed to survive but was in a complete state of shock. He had watched the bodies of his parents and six other family members cremated. The boy sat that entire night outside the cremation ground on the banks of the river Shipra.

The next morning, when Gurudev was coming out of the river after a bath, he had seen the boy. He would not speak and did not even remember his name. Gurudev had taken him under his care after renaming him as Acharya and had guided him since then.

Chanakya noticed that Acharya had a very muscular body with a 5 foot 6-inch tall frame. His dark black eyes and long dark hair that was falling over his back made him look like a sadhu. But his long white dress made him look more like a priest. He used a 5-foot bamboo reed as a walking stick.

Chanakya's introduction was not necessary as Gurudev had done justice to it in Acharya's presence.

Their travelling companions were three families who formed a group of 21 people of the farming community from the village Akasoda in Ujjain.

They were also accompanied by a group of 18 yoga teachers, artists and musicians who were also headed for Ujjain. A 24-year-old Yogini was the leader of this group. All of them had come for Gurudev's *darshan* like they did every time Gurudev came from *Padma Dham*.

The 810-km journey from Prayag to Akasoda would take them 12 days by foot.

As they proceeded, he had noticed that there were no fruit trees along the path on which they were moving. So, the first thing he wanted to know was about growing fruit trees along the path, so that the fruits could be eaten by the future travellers and the needy.

To achieve this objective, when they halted at the first stop, Acharya had his bamboo walking stick modified at a workshop.

It now had a simple mechanism - a pointed cone at the bottom, a cap on the top, both of which were held by springs. The bamboo stick had been hollowed, and a rod inserted in the centre connected the cap with the cone at the bottom. It was more like a ballpoint pen mechanism. The only difference was that every time the cap was pressed, the bottom cone would move down, make a hole in the ground and deposit some balls made of seed, mud and manure through two slots on opposite sides of the stick and plant them into the ground. Acharya would then cover the cone formed in the ground with some soil and sprinkle some water over it. The accompanying farmers had also assured him that nature would eventually help in converting some of these seeds into trees. Acharya was determined to grow fruit bearing trees all along the way!

As they were having food during a break, four puppies came and started playing with Acharya. He fed them with some rice he was having as they seemed very hungry and their mother was nowhere around. Once they resumed their journey, these four puppies started following him. They would be his companions for the rest of their life.

Acharya spent time talking with his fellow travellers all along. From these talks, both Acharya and Chanakya got to know that the main concern of the farmers was ensuring that they had enough food to eat. Besides, regular water supply for irrigation was always an issue. Additionally, the children never got any good education.

The other group described to them how they were dedicated to ensuring yoga, music and cultural traditions were kept alive. They informed Acharya and Chanakya how Yogini was involved in spreading these. This group operated from a school set up by Yogini's grandfather in Ujjain. They were now very keen to learn from Acharya the things he had learnt at *Padma Dham* and wanted to spread these pearls of wisdom as well to people.

Finally, twelve days after they had begun their journey, they arrived in Ujjain. Yogini's group parted ways with the farmers near the *Shree Kala Bhairarav* Temple.

Acharya, Chanakya and the farmers now started travelling south, passed the *Mahakaleshwar Jyotirlinga* Temple and finally reached their destination at Akasoda village late in the evening.

Life at *Padma Dham*

Padma Dham was a magical place for Ashoka - just as it was for all the residents there. He found that there were many residents who had come here from various parts of the globe and were obviously from different backgrounds.

Gurudev had informed Ashoka that there used to be many places like *Padma Dham* in the Himalayas earlier. Over a period, many of these had to be abandoned due to various reasons. However, *Padma Dham* survived, but was not accessible to most people and thus remained isolated. Many seers and seekers belonging to various traditions from many places that had to be abandoned had found refuge here. This had led to a mingling of various traditions at *Padma Dham*.

Ashoka had been instructed by Gurudev to wake up much before sunrise, have his bath and then start with his yoga practices and meditation.

Gurudev educated Ashoka on the importance and significance of the twilight in the *Sanathana Dharma*. "The time before the sunrise and the time during the sunset are considered extremely auspicious. The time before the sunlight removes the darkness of the night, and the time before light makes way for darkness in the sky are the best occasions for meditation."

"The inhalation during breathing is likened to life and the exhalation is likened to death. While doing *Pranayama* that involved various breathing techniques, a student has to try and observe the short gap between the inhalation and exhalation. Similarly, the light giving way for darkness and vice-versa could be likened to the gap between inhalation and exhalation," Gurudev shared.

Outside *Padma Dham* were cave entrances in each of the eight directions. Each of these entrances was camouflaged to avoid unnecessary visitors interrupting the residents here.

The people from surrounding villages who were familiar with these entrances used to stock goat milk, cow milk, fruits, nuts, various cereals like barley and wheat in addition to various roots.

Ashoka had to also learn the intricate and confusing paths that led the residents out of *Padma Dham* through a network of caves to reach these cave mouths which connected *Padma Dham* to the outside world.

As Ashoka was the youngest resident of *Padma Dham*, he was tasked with collecting the various food offerings of the villagers and distributing the same to all the residents of *Padma Dham*.

He would start with the collection of these offerings from the East, keep all these at the central circular gap between the banyan and the other five large trees, and then move in the clockwise direction, finally ending up collecting the offerings at the North-East.

He would then make the first offering of goat milk and some fruits to Gurudev and then proceed to keep the various offerings outside the caves where seekers and seers stayed. These residents would tell him of things that he should keep as per the diet requirements of their current practices, in addition to their water requirements. If any cooking needed to be done, each of the individual residents would do it by themselves.

Any discarded food would be used as fertilisers for the plants. All the excess dry food would then be stored in a large common cave. This storage cave had a circular enclosure at the centre where a fire used to burn continuously. All the light-coloured aromatic smoke from the burning of the twigs and herbs used here, would rise inside the cave and escape through a small opening in the high ceiling. This cave was also used to store the firewood and the herbs collected for burning.

Once Ashoka would finish these activities, he would be guided by Gurudev on *Shruti Scriptures* which included the wisdom of the *Vedas*. Gurudev would recite the *Samhita* hymns or *Mantras* and it would then be repeated by Ashoka. This was followed by a commentary by Gurudev. Many of the other residents who wanted to learn these *Shruti Scriptures* would be a part of the group. Some of them would attend these sessions just for the purpose of being in Gurudev's presence.

Ashoka loved water and whenever he had free time, he would dip himself in the cold water or shower himself under the waterfall. The spring water was extremely hot at the centre and many of the residents here used it to cook their food. However, at the points where the cold water flowed from the East and North-east into this circular enclosure, the temperature was just right and Ashoka used it to have a relaxing hot water bath.

He would also love to roam around on the hills of *Padma Dham* in addition to the wild areas surrounding it.

Ashoka learnt that there were many seers and masters in addition to the seekers who were staying in *Padma Dham*. Gurudev had clearly told that they should not be disturbed. If Ashoka needed to learn from them, Gurudev would guide him to them or that these Masters would approach Ashoka.

One day, a seer called Vaidya muni approached Ashoka. He was very old and asked him to help him in his activities. Vaidya muni was an expert in *Ayurveda*, the ancient medicinal science. While assisting him, Ashoka learnt to identify various herbs, roots and other medicines. Additionally, Vaidya muni started teaching Ashoka about the principles of *Ayurveda*.

Ashoka knew that the words *Ayur* and *Veda* meant Life and Knowledge. Thus, *Ayurveda* is a Science of the 'Knowledge of Life.'

Vaidya muni educated Ashoka - "This is an ancient form of holistic medicine and healing practice. Central to its understanding is that life is a combination of body and its senses, mind, and soul and that nothing exists without the preexistence of *Paramatma* (the Supreme Soul)."

He taught Ashoka how *Ayurveda* seeks to know and heal based on the understanding that this supreme soul expresses through various aspects of life.

"The functioning of all matter can be understood as the interactions of three fundamental energies. These three energies are: *Vata,* the dynamic or mobile, energetic; *Pitta,* the nonmaterial aspect of nature, the transformative, intelligence aspect; and *Kapha,* the structural, physical aspect," explained Vaidya Muni.

Ashoka would accompany Vaidya Muni to collect the material required for making medicines from within *Padma Dham* or from outside. He would also assist in preparing the medicines required. Ashoka understood that healing was not possible only by these medicines. Healing came from a much deeper understanding and practice. He would observe that sometimes Vaidya Muni could heal wounds or cure people in the villages around *Padma Dham* just by his touch.

Gurudev once directed Ashoka to learn *Tummo* and other techniques from Tilopa, a Tibetan monk residing there. *Tummo* literally meant 'Internal fire.' He learnt a combination of breathing techniques accompanied by meditation methods which helped him generate enough body heat to withstand the cold temperatures at *Padma Dham*. This was just the beginning. At the end of three years, Ashoka had learnt more advanced practices like *Trul Khor*. This helped Ashoka gain mastery over body movements as well as his breathing and eventually assisted him in meditation.

Tilopa had said, "*Trul Khor* is one of the most revered and secret practices of our tradition that has 108 steps. These are a combination of dynamic body postures or *Asanas*, recitation of *Mantras*, *Pranayama* and various visualisations."

Bhaskara was a 30-year-old Astronomer and Cosmologist who had come back to India from Europe to study the ancient Astrology. He felt that his core expertise would help advance and update the ancient science of Astrology that had not kept up with the advancements in modern Astronomy. He came to know of Gurudev and decided to stay at *Padma Dham* and pursue his learning of

Astrology from the masters and the ancient texts available here.

Bhaskara had carried a small telescope to *Padma Dham*. He had set up his observatory in one of the caves which was at a higher altitude. This cave had lost its ceiling and was open to the sky for most part except where the dome met the floor on the circumference of this circular cave. This opening was above three feet in height from the cave floor. Thus a very wide viewing angle available for astronomical observation from horizon to horizon. Ashoka loved to watch the stars in these clear skies using this telescope. Bhaskara showed Ashoka how the cave they were observing from resembled the meteor-impact craters on the moon.

On one of the nights, Bhaskara spoke to him about the Big Bang Theory. Once Bhaskara had finished, Ashoka recalled an age-old story about the Primordial Universe he had heard repeatedly from the *Prajapati* potters. According to them the vessels 'Kumbha' and 'Kalasha' mirror the creation which takes place in the Primordial cosmic universe. He had just learnt from Bhaskara about the shape of the Universe as it expanded from a single point. He agreed that there was a slight resemblance of the pottery vessels to what science says about the initial expanding universe. However, he was not sure if the potters were right or were the modern sciences that were accurate or whether both of these were correct in their own different ways.

His curiosity eventually led him to learn about the non-terrestrial objects in the sky, the various constellations, and he eventually learnt the inter-connectedness of matter, energy, space and time.

As he was learning modern astronomy, Bhaskara also taught him the mathematics and the basics of ancient astrology.

After about six years of stay at *Padma Dham*, Ashoka started learning *Upanishads* from Gurudev. Ashoka had learnt that the word *Upanishad* meant receiving the highest wisdom by sitting near a Guru. This was accompanied by periods of solitude in caves for meditation on the ultimate truths that he had learnt.

Various other Seers at *Padma Dham* also taught Ashoka different aspects of wisdom from their ancient and traditional texts.

After seven years, Ashoka's stay at *Padma Dham* had come to an end, and it seemed to him that time had flown by.

Gurudev told Ashoka that they would have to visit 'The Nine' before they proceeded for the *Maha Kumbha Mela* at Haridwar.

The Nine

Before leaving for the *Maha Kumbha Mela*, Gurudev told Ashoka that he would have to meet 'The Nine'. Ashoka was very inquisitive as who were they and what was the purpose of this meeting. The only thing Gurudev informed him was that they had called for Ashoka, and one very rarely gets to hear of them. Even Gurudev had been called only once.

The next day, just after sunrise, Gurudev and Ashoka started their journey. They exited *Padma Dham* from one of the caves in the South-East. Gurudev informed him, "This journey will take us two days, and we have to travel in the south-east direction. We will travel only when the sun is visible in the sky and rest when it gets dark."

As the day was to end, Gurudev pointed to a conically shaped mountain cap and told Ashoka that it was their destination. Ashoka saw that it was unique not only because of its shape but also because it could be distinguished easily from far, as the ice on the mountain seemed to give it a distinctive crystal look.

As it was about to get dark, they decided to put up for the night in a small cave on the way.

The next morning, at sunrise, they resumed their journey. It took them three hours to reach the base of this conically shaped mountain.

On reaching the base, Gurudev sat on a small rock and pointed in the direction of a small entrance to the cave. Gurudev then told Ashoka, "You now have to go in there alone as whatever 'The Nine' have to say is meant for you and you alone. I will have no part in this."

Ashoka approached the cave opening and saw a path. He saw that this pathway was lined with ice and the way it reflected light he thought it was a crystal formation lining these walls. The natural light from outside reflected perfectly on the winding path, clearly revealing the way into the cave. As he walked, he started feeling a rush of intense energy that seemed to increase with every step he took forward. Ashoka was amazed that even after he had walked for about nine minutes on the snaky pathway, the light seemed to reflect perfectly and was guiding him deep inside.

Suddenly, he saw a blinding white light. In a reflex action, he closed his eyes and blocked them with his palms while his neck turned in the other direction. He was in total awe.

Once he had recovered from this shock, he slowly moved his head in the direction he was earlier moving while keeping his eyes still covered with his hands. He could still feel the light and didn't gather the courage to either open his eyes or remove the hands covering them. As he saw downwards, the pathway now looked slightly darker and everything around was brighter. He knew instinctively that he had to move with his eyes closed and hands protecting the eyes.

He started moving along the path cautiously, maintaining his balance as he walked. His body felt so light that he felt as if he was walking in a dream.

When he had walked a little further, he could now see the bright lights in the shape of nine humans sitting on a common platform. He recognised these as 'The Nine.'

"Who could they be?" he wondered.

"We are called 'The Nine,' and we are human souls liberated from the cycle of Life and Death. Ever since the first human was liberated, there has been a tradition of guiding the rest on this path. Nine enlightened souls remain on this earth without wearing a body. We remain connected to the 'Infinite,' but we are not fully merged. The compassion of 'The Nine' helps guide the seekers as well as the non-seekers to the ultimate goal of life."

Someone had answered his question.

Ashoka now wondered if 'The Nine' communicated through thoughts. He immediately got his answer. "Yes. We send thoughts to one specific person to communicate.

Sometimes we even send out a thought which is not directed at one person but will be received by one or many bodies."

"If they could easily transmit thoughts to him, why was he called here?"

His thoughts got a prompt reply, "You have been told by Gurudev about the role you have to play in the transition of the *Yugas*. He has also prepared your body and mind for this path you will take. However, you will require much more which you will receive with your presence here. Hence, you had to come with your body here. Your being is to be prepared for the eventualities you have to face."

As he listened to these thoughts, he observed that each communication seemed to come from one of 'The Nine.' It was as if one of them was speaking with him at a time and his head would automatically face the one speaking with him.

The one in the centre started conversing with him. "You have worn various bodies in the past and have now finally reached this critical stage. You obviously do not remember any of this as you shed off all the matter when you leave each body. With each death, all that mattered is also lost. That includes all of your thoughts, desires and wishes."

He immediately started seeing the different lives he had lived as if he was watching it like he was an observer.

Every moment of every life he had lived started flashing across him now. Finally, his previous life as Emperor Ashokavardhana Maurya passed before him.

He could not even comprehend what he just saw. Also, every moment of what he just witnessed was now etched in his memory. It was as if he could now recall every moment of all of his earlier births.

He was not sure how long he had now been in this cave. He realised that whatever reason he had been called for was over now and it was time to leave.

Ashoka fell flat on his belly prostrating before 'The Nine' to seek their blessing. He was still keeping his eyes closed with his hands firmly on them.

With their permission and blessings, he slowly started moving out of the cave along the winding path. When the blinding light disappeared on the way out, the sunlight started guiding him to the entrance of the cave.

He saw Gurudev open his eyes from the meditation as he approached the rock outside the cave. Gurudev blessed him, and they started moving in the direction of Haridwar.

Vishwakarma

Vishwakarma was born in Sompura in Gujarat. His parents Agastya and Aditi belonged to a *Shilpi* family. *Shilpis* are traditional sculptors and are well-known for their great artistic work on wood, stones and metals. This family was known for their stone carvings for many generations.

By the age of 15, Vishwakarma had mastered the art of stone sculpting using soft stones like marble and harder stones like sandstone and even granite. As was the tradition, he had been trained in the various aspects of ancient sciences and art related to sculpting including *Vaastu Vidya* and *Vaastu Shastra*. Additionally, he also learnt the knowledge of the family's otherwise secrets and history of many generations.

He developed a fascination to learn about the historical stone sculptures and structures created across the globe. His fascination turned to obsession when he realised that no one could explain how some of these structures were made. It was as if some chapters of human ingenuity had been erased by the cruel ravages of time. However, these creations in stone were staring in the face of people challenging them to unravel the sciences behind their creation.

He started to connect with various knowledgeable people and experts across the globe to learn more, but this didn't help him. Some offbeat explanations like the use of some form of energy seemed to make sense to him.

Thus began Vishwakarma's learning of the various energy forms. He started his Masters and went on to do Doctoral research in the field of Electromagnetic Spectrum.

At the end of his study, he had a thorough insight into the various known forms of energy. He also learnt how the various forms of energy had been put to different uses by humans. However, the answer to how it could have been used to create large stone monuments and that too with such great precision still eluded him.

During this time, he had availed every opportunity to improve and master his stone sculpting skills by learning more and more traditional techniques that were not indigenous to his native place of Sompura.

The day of his doctoral convocation was the most frustrating day. He had not learnt anything related to his passion but at the same time, he had known a lot about all known forms of energy. He came back home after the convocation ceremony and took a hammer and a few chisels and started doing what he loved the most. Sculpting was helping him as a stress buster. He was fully engrossed in slowly removing the unwanted chips and trying to recreate something from the past.

When he was finished, he looked at the miniature of a part of Puma Puncu.

Puma Puncu is part of a large temple complex that is part of the Tiwanaku archaeological site in Western Bolivia. He recalled that Tiwanaku was a marvel in stones with large blocks of Sandstone and Andesite weighing up to 400 tons. These blocks of stone had been moved from two different quarry locations to construct this complex. The stone blocks were notched and then fitted together so that they interlocked in all the three spatial dimensions. These miracles in stone were strong enough to withstand the frequent earthquakes there. What was more amazing, these stones had no chisel marks and the means by which they were shaped was a mystery.

His gaze went back to the miniature form he had just completed in granite. A shadow now falling on it distracted his attention. The shadow belonged to a large man with an unusually bright smiling face. This stranger had been silently observing Vishwakarma for a long time.

This smiling stranger introduced himself and spent the rest of the afternoon in some small talk. He left as the sun was about to set.

Talking with this stranger had helped Vishwakarma forget his frustration.

Next morning, when he was about to start work on his stone sculpture, he again saw this stranger who had called himself Ravi. The topic of discussion today moved from stone carvings to energy. Vishwakarma was surprised about the depth of knowledge Ravi had in the subject.

This routine continued even on the third day. Vishwakarma now opened up to Ravi about his frustration about not being able to rediscover the ancient secrets. "You probably need to learn much more in depth," Ravi said and started a volley of questions directed at him.

Every day for the next three months, Vishwakarma would look forward to meeting Ravi. Every question or suggestion from Ravi seemed to magically open a new door in Vishwakarma's understanding.

When Ravi informed at the end of three months that he had to move away from Sompura the next day, Vishwakarma was dejected at first. These 90 days of interactions had helped him understand energy better than what the formal education had taught him. Not just that, he had begun to understand the very nature of all vibrations.

He needed a great laboratory to test his new understanding. So, the next three years were spent in post-doctoral studies.

At the end of three years, he had confirmed all of his understanding by testing it repeatedly on different types of stones. He had unravelled this long-lost knowledge and much more.

He was convinced that he could build mountains as big as Sagarmatha (Mount Everest) or very easily convert them to the mineral dust they were formed from. Vishwakarma knew this knowledge was dangerous, and he had to guard it against falling into the wrong hands. At the same time, it would be a pity if humanity were to lose this knowledge again.

His postdoctoral thesis didn't give even the slightest hint of this awareness.

He now longed to badly meet with Ravi to express his gratitude.

He remembered that, during one of the conversations, Ravi had told him about how he loved visiting *Kumbha Melas*. The year was 2021, and he knew that *Maha Kumbha Mela* at Haridwar was at hand. He packed up some clothes and tools to move to Haridwar.

He fondly recalled how the round bright face with brownish-red long, curly hair looked at him from a higher level as Vishwakarma sat down on the ground chipping the stone with his hammer and chisel. An innocent question would then pop out of Ravi's thick red lips. He was sure that with every one of those innocent questions from Ravi, a small chip of ignorance had left him. Finally, in 90 days and after subtly removing of lots of unwanted ignorance, Ravi had left Vishwakarma fully sculpted.

He recalled one of the phrases repeated often by Ravi, "The Sun gives us much more than life. It also helps preserve all the life on our Earth. When one looks beyond these things that are very apparent, one will start understanding that it is much more than a nuclear reactor of our Solar System taking us on a Universal journey. One only has to develop the perception and that comes only with sensitivity. This sensitivity is clearly beyond the reach of most."

Vishwakarma smiled and was more eager than before to thank Ravi for being there for him when he so desperately needed help.

Acharya's Gurukul

Ujjain is one of the oldest known places in India. It was here the first Zero Longitude was marked around the 4th Century BCE.

Akasoda is a small village about 21 kilometers from Ujjain with a total population of about 1350, and here everyone knew each other. It had about 210 children.

Acharya and Chanakya learnt that there was a small school which provided education to these kids. The teaching was mediocre and the kids preferred to play or were forced to help their parents than get educated.

Acharya and Chanakya along with Yogini discussed with the village elders about ways to improve the education of the kids and drew up a plan to start their work here.

Within three weeks, a routine had been set up at the local community hall. One of Yogini's teachers would start the day at 6 am with the teaching of Yoga. An hour later, Acharya would start with the education of Sanskrit and teach a little of Vedas. Finally, Chanakya would coach them on ancient logic and *Arthashastra*. Elders and kids would attend these sessions. The kids would then proceed to attend a formal school post their breakfast and other routine activities.

Whenever Acharya taught the Vedas, he noticed that one of the four dogs who were his companions would take turns to sit near his feet and listen to him attentively. He started addressing each of them based on the name of Veda they were attracted to.

Chanakya would spend the day helping educate the school teachers. Acharya and Chanakya would later work to understand more about the needs of the surrounding villages with the help of their patrons in Akasoda.

In about a year, the children had started using their afternoon time to learn various skills. A group of children would learn various aspects of agriculture, while some would go to learn from a cobbler or even learn construction of buildings and roads.

In the evenings, children would play. Newer sports were being introduced in Akasoda now.

In the late evenings, some volunteers from Yogini's school took up the task of teaching and performing dramas and music. This formed the basis of learning about various *Puranas* or historical stories to all the villagers, in addition to various arts.

In the seven years since Acharya and Chanakya first came to Akasoda, they had established a fairly regular schedule for the education and all-round development of the kids and the adults.

Mornings would start by learning the different aspects of yoga.

Sanskrit lessons would follow with some aspects from the Vedas or *Shruti* that was the age-old wisdom to be heard from a guru and repeated by the pupils.

Third would be a discourse on *Upavedas* which included practical application of knowledge learnt and lessons on various types of logic.

Formal schooling included learning the modern sciences, mathematics and some local and foreign languages.

Afternoons were dedicated to learning various skills which were necessary for their day to day life.

Early evenings were spent by the kids in outdoor games.

Finally, the late evenings were utilised for *Smriti* or Knowledge that has to be remembered. This included various arts and dramas which would be performed to convey the message. During this period an element of amusement would be introduced to drive home some points better.

Chanakya taught some exciting aspects of modern sciences in addition to many practical applications for the day-to-day use of the villagers.

Chanakya also started teaching some selected students how to make robots of birds, insects and crawling worms and make them appear real. These replica machines had the ability to move around just like their real-life counterparts.

More and more people with different expertise were now coming to impart their knowledge at these Gurukuls. They would come after learning about the Gurukul from the villagers or from the Yogini's school or from Chanakya's network.

Whenever the villagers required any help, this group at Acharya's Gurukul would find ways of solving their problems.

One such example was the water shortage. Water for irrigation was a continuous problem. Small wells, ponds and lakes were dug up with the help of all villagers. These water bodies were connected by small channels and it was eventually ensured that there would be no water shortage. Groundwater replenishment was taught to these villagers. The government also contributed by expediting the phase-2 of Narmada-Shipra linking project which ensured sufficient supply of the water.

Finally, when it was time for the 2021 *Maha Kumbha Mela*, Acharya, along with Chanakya, proceeded towards Haridwar.

108 Gurukuls were now functioning for 972 villages. This meant that one Gurukul was available for nine villages on an average.

Nava Grahas

2400 years before the present time, Kautilya sat in self-isolation in his room at Takshashila. Takshashila was the greatest University of learning on Earth and Kautilya was one of the most well-known teachers' here. His pupils had learnt his *Arthashashtra,* the most popular treatises on Political Science and Economics from him. Some of his disciples had accompanied him to Pataliputra in far off Magadha and had seen him being insulted by the King Dhana Nanda. In addition to being their teacher, they regarded him as an extremely intelligent person, who had pledged to finish the rule of Dhana Nanda and his Nanda Dynasty.

Today was the ninth day of his self-isolation and his disciples were now getting worried. They knew he was not known for brooding. However, what they did not know was that Kautilya had taken upon himself another task that he would eventually share with only a handful of his disciples. Kautilya also knew that he had to complete this equally important task before he moved east to ensure the destruction of the Nanda Dynasty and the eventual integration of Bhaarata. He now had his plan ready.

The threat from the West was now very real and there were armies waiting to invade and plunder *Bhaarata*. Takshashila University had great secrets and valuable ancient knowledge that had been passed on for thousands of years by the teachers to the most deserving students. In order to ensure that this knowledge is preserved for eternity, he chose nine of his most trusted disciples. They were each go on to learn this valuable knowledge in their field of expertise and would eventually be called the '*Nava Grahas.*'

This name was inspired by the '*Nava Grahas*' of Astrology. Ancient Astrology has '*Nava Grahas*' that are nine non-terrestrial or celestial bodies which have their influences on Earth and life on Earth. These include seven physical bodies that can be observed in the sky. The other two of these nine are non-physical and hence cannot be observed and yet influence the life on Earth.

These nine men or '*Nava Grahas*' were tasked by Kautilya with the mission of passing this knowledge to their most deserving students and to ensure preservation of this invaluable knowledge. They also had to ensure that this knowledge is upgraded while ensuring it is hidden from undeserving people. This meant that they would eventually work in the shadows. These '*Nava Grahas*' were hence more popularly referred as the 'Nine Unknown Men.'

Before Kautilya's passing away, he ensured that the control of these *'Nava Grahas'* was passed on to his grandson Radhagupta.

Radhagupta eventually became the minister of Bindusara and also of Ashokavardhana, the second and third Emperors of the Mauryan dynasty.

Radhagupta passed the control of these *'Nava Grahas'* to Ashokavardhana before dying.

There was always a great danger of this invaluable knowledge falling into wrong hands. Hence, Emperor Ashokavardhana did not want these nine men to meet each other. They would communicate with him in an ancient language in which the manuscripts of *'Nava Grahas'* were written. They would also encode all their acquired knowledge in this same unknown language. In addition, he ensured that they worked in obscurity, not revealing their identity to anyone. All this would eventually form the basis of their secrecy code. Each of the newly initiated successors of *'Nava Grahas'*, would additionally learn about the lineage through which the knowledge was passed.

Before Ashokavardhana's death, he ensured that the *'Nava Grahas'* would not be controlled by anyone but would work independently. They would also never attempt to meet or even acknowledge the presence of the other eight members. However, they would help each other incognito by physically not revealing their identity in the eventuality of any danger to any of the nine. Their distress calls would be communicated in their secret language.

Ashoka was in Gurudev's tent at Haridwar. The *Maha Kumbha Mela* of 2021 had got over, and everyone had left for their destinations. Ashoka had informed that he would stay in Haridwar for a week and would join Acharya after that.

Ever since Ashoka had reached Haridwar for the *Maha Kumbha Mela*, he had been going around Haridwar whenever Gurudev allowed him. He used every opportunity to face an enthusiastic journalist wanting to record and report the spectacle at Haridwar. One thing each of these journalists didn't understand was the language in which he spoke when they asked him any question. They also never gave much thought to the gibberish he spoke as they were busy and had to rush to report the next spectacle.

Sunday morning, Ashoka had finished his meditation and *asanas* after his bath in the river Ganga and was seated where Gurudev had sat all these days.

A visitor arrived in this tent and a verbal exchange happened between the two. Once Ravi (the Sun) had confirmed the authenticity of the teenager, he came and stood in front of Ashoka. Ravi bowed down and placed a thick manuscript with a red cover at Ashoka's feet. On top of this, he placed a large 3"-diameter red ruby and then proceeded to sit in front of him.

The next hours were spent in long discussion on how Ravi and his predecessors had worked as per the guidelines set since the time of Emperor Ashokavardhana. They had ensured the spread of light. In fact, they had devoted their lives to guide humanity to understand different forms of energy step by step and also recognise the effects of these on humans and other aspects of nature. He explained how, at every stage, the human brain always had tried to use the new learning for destruction and how, at every stage, they had to be patient not to intervene but simply watch from the background as per their code.

Ashoka informed Ravi of the role Gurudev had played in training him. He also broadly told him about his plans to prepare the humans for upcoming *Satya Yuga*.

He wanted Ravi to help hasten the training of deserving students from Acharya's Gurukul. He would provide instructions to Ravi on the help that would be required.

On Monday morning, Chandra (Moon) appeared and repeated the same exercise. Chandra had placed a large pearl on the manuscript with a silvery white cover. Chandra described the progress of humanity in the field of small which included colloidal matter, microbiology, physics of particles, genetics and now was slowly moving into nanotechnology.

On the same day, at sunset, Rahu (the Northern Lunar Node) came and placed an orange-brown hessonite garnet with a manuscript having the similar colour. Rahu explained how men had been guided steadily in physiology with the methods of identifying and curing of ailments and how modern medicine had been developed. Rahu also explained how the known techniques of using various *Marmas* (seats of life or pressure points of the body) to cause unconsciousness, death, chronic lesions, etc. had been taught to very few individuals and had been almost lost now. Rahu also explained how the understanding of the resurrection of humans and other life forms after their death had been restricted to very few yogis.

Mangala (Mars) entered the tent on Tuesday morning and proceeded to keep a large coral with a manuscript below it near Ashoka's feet, before sitting down in front of him. Mangala went on to explain to Ashoka how the art of war and the knowledge of weaponry has been slowly revealed to humanity. Mangala also revealed how during most of the history, humans have still created havoc with the crudest of weapons available to them. However, the nuclear weapons knowledge had brought about some semblance of fragile peace. Mangala went on to add that they are slowly learning how to create deterrence for the most powerful weapons known to them. Mangala was confident that humans have to evolve significantly to receive the knowledge of most potent weapons that had created ultimate losses of life and destruction across solar systems and galaxies in the past.

Wednesday brought Budha (Mercury) who placed an emerald on the green cover of his manuscript at Ashoka's feet. Budha described how mass opinions have been moulded to change the course of humanity. He also described how some individuals in the course of the last 2300 years had been gradually taught the use of propaganda and psychological warfare while enabling them to govern and establish order across the world.

Guru (Jupiter) came on Thursday and placed a yellow sapphire on a matching yellow covered manuscript. Guru talked about how the knowledge of transformation of substances had developed into the various sciences. Guru also described how Alchemy and the metamorphosis of substances along with the understanding of their esoteric properties had been taught to only a select few in dire need and now it was known to none.

Shukra (Venus) arrived on Friday with a large diamond on top of his manuscript. Shukra gave a detailed narration on how transportation had been gradually upgraded. He also talked about how communication methods had been changed step by step to the present. He also went on to add how humanity was still not prepared for extraterrestrial communication or teleportation even though the ideas had been planted more than a century ago.

It was Shani (Saturn) on Saturday morning with a blue sapphire kept on a matching cover of the manuscript. Shani conversed with Ashoka on how the secrets of gravitation were being slowly revealed across the last six centuries and how the *Vaiminaka Shastra* which dealt with the science of flying objects had gradually been revealed in the last century. Shani was sure that the humanity was a long way from Intergalactic travel and before that they would have to be taught the true nature of gravity, bit by bit.

Finally, on Saturday evening, Ketu (the Southern Lunar Node) came and placed a large cat's eye gemstone with the manuscript at Ashoka's feet. Ketu had a discussion on how baby steps have been taken by humans in understanding the complexity of Cosmology and in knowing the basics of the nature of space-time. Ketu felt that humans were just in the kindergarten stage and that they had a very long way to go before they mature enough to understand the multi-dimensional and multi-universe nature.

Ashoka had told each of the 'Nava Grahas' that his rules of engagement would remain the same with them in the sense that he would not be controlling them. However, he wanted each of them to identify and prepare 81 potential candidates instead of the 9 earlier. Of these 81 experts created, nine would become 'Upagrahas' (satellites).

Each of these 'Upagrahas' would be prepared in the dissemination of the next knowledge to humans. Once prepared, the 'Nava Grahas' along with the 'Upagrahas' would help disseminate this new knowledge and guide humanity in their own different ways.

Eventually, one of these *'Upagrahas'* would become a *'Nava Grahas'* when the time came. He explained that this modification was necessary as the times would be turbulent during the change of the *Yugas*.

Finally, when Ashoka was alone in the tent, he was happy that *'Nava Grahas'* had done a great service to humanity, by gradually disseminating the knowledge. He was also happy about the role of women in this. He was delighted that five of the *'Nava Grahas'* were now women.

However, the way this understanding was being put to use by humans disturbed him. He also shuddered at the thought of humanity having all this knowledge with their present inadequate level of awareness and maturity.

Vishwakarma at Haridwar

Vishwakarma had reached Haridwar after the *Maha Kumbha Mela* had already started. He was stunned by the huge gathering of humanity in this holy place.

He spent his time visiting various temples trying to understand how they had sculpted these using various types of stones. What surprised him was that most of these temples had been reconstructed as all the ancient ones had been destroyed by the foreign barbarians plundering these places. He felt that they should have been reconstructed entirely in stone without desecrating them with concrete and steel.

He would spend more of his time walking along the sacred river Ganga trying to gauge how she had sculpted the surroundings over centuries and millennia as she gracefully slid down on the surface of the earth.

When he got exhausted, he would sit or lie down on the river bank or on one of the hills overlooking the river.

On one of the days, he walked about 21 kilometres to Rishikesh and came back to Haridwar when he had fully explored the place for a few days.

One day, he suddenly realised that the *Maha Kumbha Mela* was coming to end when he saw the crowds dwindling rapidly and the tents disappearing slowly.

He had still not been able to meet Ravi. The thought was disappointing as he was sure that he would have easily recognised Ravi even from among a billion people. There were only a couple of million people here, and he had not yet met with success.

As usual, when he was seated on the riverbank in the morning, he suddenly recognised the familiar face he was so eagerly looking forward to seeing. As soon as he saw the bright smiling face and the curly reddish hair, he jumped with ecstasy. As he approached Ravi, the familiar semicircle above the two eyebrows representing the rising Sun made from sandalwood paste and the surrounding perpendicular red lines became very clear.

He bowed down to Ravi and excitedly told him of his progress and profusely thanked him for all the guidance.

Ravi informed Vishwakarma, "This is very dangerous knowledge and has to be hidden from most of the humanity." Ravi then smiled as if to say that he was aware of all that had happened in his learning. This reaction perplexed him. However, what Ravi did next was even more extraordinary.

Ravi pointed to one of the few remaining tents where the sadhus were supposed to have stayed. He said, "You are now ready to meet someone who will give direction to your life henceforth."

When they entered the tent, Vishwakarma saw only a teenage boy sitting on a platform in the tent. Ravi bowed down to this boy and then sat near his feet. Ravi then pointed to Vishwakarma and told the boy about him. It was strange for Vishwakarma to see the reverence Ravi had for this young boy. Finally, Ravi explained how Vishwakarma would be useful to Ashoka.

Ashoka knew that Vishwakarma was safer with him especially in the light of the forbidden knowledge he had acquired. He was also pleased that within a week of his meeting with Ravi, a perfect substitute for Ravi had come to his doorstep and Vishwakarma could help a lot in the direction they were moving in.

Even though Ashoka felt that Ravi could now include Vishwakarma as an *Upagraha*, he said nothing and left the decision to Ravi.

Once he had learnt enough, Ashoka described to Vishwakarma how Gurudev had tasked him with the responsibility of ensuring people are prepared for the transitioning of the *Yugas*. He went on to explain how Acharya and Chanakya had set up the Gurukuls. He also went on to describe how lots of help was required as the task given was simply a mammoth one.

All along when Ashoka spoke, Vishwakarma felt the grace of a leader and forcefulness of a lion in him. If he were to sculpt a statue of Ashoka, he was sure that it had to have the looks of a lion. Ravi also seemed to be in awe as he heard this teenager's voice. Vishwakarma was now sure that this was a very powerful person whom he could not help but admire. He also knew that the task given to Ashoka was one in which the end was nowhere to be seen. He wondered how anyone could be given such a responsibility knowing fully that it was impossible to accomplish all of this in a lifetime. Vishwakarma also knew he could play a role in helping Ashoka achieve his goal, and he offered to be at his side.

One thing Vishwakarma would never understand was why Ravi was so devoted to this young teenager. He would not understand this connection for a long time to come.

Ujjain

On their way to Ujjain, Ashoka described in detail to Vishwakarma how Acharya and Chanakya had set up Gurukuls in and around Ujjain.

In the preceding years, Acharya and Chanakya had set up 108 Gurukuls which covered 972 villages. This meant that an average of nine villages was covered by one the Gurukuls. It was a great achievement by these two. However, Ashoka also wanted these Gurukuls to spread across the nation quickly.

The route took them 12 days on foot. They were pleasantly surprised that there were plenty of fruit trees all along the way, and they would have a variety of fruits for all their meals. It was later after they reached Ujjain, they would learn that these were the fruits of Acharya's wisdom and hard work.

All along, Vishwakarma had been wondering how he could help Ashoka in setting up new Gurukuls. He had more or less formulated a plan. He now wished Ravi was here to guide him and bridge many of the gaps in his blueprint. However, after reaching Akasoda and meeting Chanakya, he was sure that both of them could easily work it out.

Vishwakarma and Chanakya laboured for 18 days and finally, they called Ashoka and others to view the marvel of their creation.

There was a large flattened circle in the centre of this structure which Vishwakarma created. Concentric circular steps rose up from this stage at a lower level. This entire structure looked as though it was carved from a single rock. Ashoka estimated that this place looked like one mini stadium and could easily house about 200 to 300 people.

They were admiring its perfectness from the outermost circle, which was at an elevation of about 9 feet from the circular stage at the bottom. This outermost circle and its outer surroundings were at the same height. It was clear to them that it looked as though a large rock had been cut into six concentric steps and the lowermost was a circular stage in the middle.

Vishwakarma assured them, "It is made of stone however not from solid rock, but from the use of energy and powdered sand." This revelation left all others stunned. This meant that Vishwakarma understood the art of creating stones and its structures from sand. They were even more surprised that this structure took less than a day to construct.

When their attention was directed to the large crystal balls on the circumference, they were surprised to see them and started wondering why crystal balls were required. Each of these balls had a different diameter. From the largest in the east as they moved clockwise along the circumference, the size of these crystal balls became smaller. There were four of them placed in the four directions.

Vishwakarma started explaining about these large spheres. "The largest sphere is a data storage device. It can pick up all the data available from different sources across the globe and store it. The second sphere is connected to it wirelessly, and it will pick-up only the relevant information from the first and stores it. Similarly, the third is a storage device for only the relevant knowledge picked up from the second orb. The fourth crystal ball is the smallest and is a storage device for the wisdom collected and generated from the third one."

"All of these transparent crystal balls are not just storage devices; they are able to process and transmit whatever is stored in them or when a device is connected to them. Additionally, they are able to pick up the energy of the Sun, use it and even store the excess energy."

Chanakya explained briefly how these were prepared layer by layer while incorporating the necessary electronics, still ensuring that they look like crystal balls through which one could see very clearly.

Then there were additional cylinders on the circular steps. Chanakya demonstrated how the entire system worked. He went to the cylinder at the heart of the stage and placed his palm on the semi-circular crystal on the top of it. This activated the entire set up. He gave a voice command to retrieve the recording of that morning's class. Immediately a three-dimensional real life-like Ashoka's class started. Chanakya explained, "These cylinders are picking up stored information from the information sphere and transmitting life-like visuals and sounds."

Next, he showed how all the knowledge and information which was available could be retrieved as a three-dimensional view even if it was stored in a two-dimensional format. These views could be enlarged to get better in-depth expanded views. "These features will help the students learn with greater clarity," Chanakya added.

Finally, all of them turned their attention to the dome-shaped transparent roof covering this structure. It would light up whenever the ambient light reduced and gave daylight like feeling in this place. It was energised by solar energy collected and stored within the same roof.

Additionally, there were rotating blades which formed the part of the eight wind turbines which would transfer the energy collected to storage on the roof. Furthermore, these rotating fans also ensured that the entire setup remained properly ventilated and pleasant to sit.

Chanakya and Vishwakarma went on to explain how this system would use its own frequency which would connect it to distant classrooms and transmit what was being taught here. Also, people from multiple places could use this system to interact with one another and still get the feeling they were at the same place. Having a separate frequency to connect to other devices ensured that it was out of bounds of all other networks.

Ashoka and Acharya were delighted as this meant that they could now expand the Gurukuls at a much faster pace.

All Chanakya and Vishwakarma would now need were some students from the Gurukul to learn to replicate this system.

The raw materials used in this entire set up were the minerals and compounds easily, freely and naturally available around them. The replication process would be taught, but not the understanding of the technologies involved. These technologies would eventually be passed only to a few deserving ones out of those students who will learn to replicate it.

Finally, it was time for Ashoka, Acharya, Chanakya and Vishwakarma to leave Ujjain.

It was decided that Chanakya and Vishwakarma would travel North-West and later continue their journey eastwards once they had reached the borders of the country, setting up Gurukuls all along.

Similarly, Ashoka and Acharya would move south along the western coast, and once they reached the southernmost tip, they would continue by moving northwards, setting up Gurukuls along the eastern coast.

Some teachers of the Gurukuls that were already set up in and around Ujjain were designated to expand the reach of Gurukuls.

Chanakya's network now also included *Kinnars* (Eunuchs or Transgenders). This network, along with the beggars, would guide all of them before they reached any place.

Ashoka installed the *Shiksha Stambha* before they left. This was a pillar signifying the re-establishment of true education.

This *Shiksha Stambha* stood tall at 18 meters. It was a grand pillar made of dark black granite with a pink lotus on top. Below the lotus were four golden Lions carved looking out in four directions. Under each of the lions were four *chakras* or wheels. Between each of these *chakras* were four different life forms – a tree, a fish, a bird and a cow. At the bottom of the pillar, were four elephants facing four directions. Above the pink lotus was a white swan.

Each of these figures implied a different aspect of education. Elephants were a sign of knowledge. The four life forms indicated respect for all of the nature.

The *chakras* denoted understanding the cyclic nature of everything. Lions meant strength. Lotus stood for the flowering of wisdom at Gurukuls. Swan symbolised the purity which comes with the capability to understand as well as reject impurity and ignorance. The granite stone that made up the pillar showed the ability of some aspects of nature to be able to stand firm and unaffected across the various *Yugas*. The carvings meant that humans were able to shape nature as they pleased. However, they should develop the intelligence and maturity to live in harmony rather than destroy it. Finally, the height signified how the aspiration of the humans on the ground attempted to reach high up to the skies.

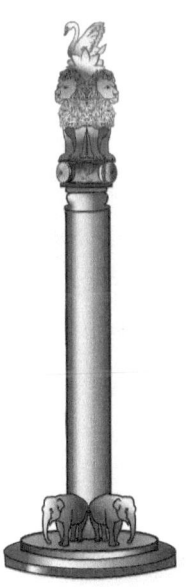

Kerala

Ashoka and Acharya moved along the western coast setting up Gurukuls along the way. They had finally reached Kerala, the southernmost state on the western coast.

Ashoka had learnt about *Dhanurvidya* or the art of fighting in one of the *Upavedas*.

Upavedas are associated with Vedas. The word *Upaveda* translates as practical or applied Knowledge. *Dhanurveda* is the *Upaveda* that details many of the weapons employed by a practitioner. The seven types of fighting that a warrior should practice and achieve proficiency in, according to the *Dhanurveda,* are Archery, Discus, Spear, Sword/Shield, Dagger, Mace (club) and bare-hand.

There are references in *Dhanurveda* to *Kalaripayattu,* an ancient martial art form, which is considered to be one of the oldest surviving forms of martial art on Earth and had originated in south of India.

Kalaripayattu is a combination of two words, namely, '*Kalari*' which means battlefield and '*Payattu*' meaning to fight. Thus, *Kalaripayattu* refers to practising the arts of the battlefield.

Bodhidharma, a south Indian prince, took Buddhism to China in the fifth century CE. The Shaolin Temple there is said to have been started by him where he taught *Kalaripayattu* to the monks there for their self-defence, which was modified by him to suit their needs and eventually was known as *Kung-fu*.

The movements and postures in the art of *Kalaripayattu* are believed to be inspired by the raw strength and movements of animals and are also named after them. There is a belief that this art was developed in the forests when hunters had observed the fighting techniques of different animals.

Ashoka was very keen to learn this art now that he was in Kozhikode in the Malabar region of Kerala.

Kozhikode is a coastal town, and for centuries it has been one of the conduits for local spices that had great demand in the western countries.

He got to know of Devi who had her Gurukul on the banks of the river Kallai. When Ashoka met Devi, he guessed that this lady with a slim frame which stood 5 feet 3 inches tall was about 60 years old. Ashoka had learnt that this woman had dedicated her entire life to teaching *Kalaripayattu* to all aspirants.

He described to Devi how he and Acharya had set up Gurukuls and had started moving south. When he told her their intention of setting up Gurukuls, she immediately offered them a piece of land adjacent to her *Kalari*. Ashoka and Acharya also had a group of students from Devi's Gurukul to start with.

The next day, Acharya and Ashoka started their routine of teaching the ancient language, the sciences and the knowledge in the morning.

Ashoka entered Devi's *Kalari* around nine in the morning. He had to walk down the steps into the *Kalari* which was built about 9 feet below the ground. The atmosphere in the *Kalari* was more like a *Mandir* or Temple. His initiation started with praying and lighting lamps and praying to Lord Parashuram who is said to have taught *Kalaripayattu* to the locals here. He then accepted Devi as his guru. He had to wear a red and white traditional dress after which his training started.

Ashoka found it fascinating to watch this guru teaching while wearing a traditional saree - he wondered how she could be so agile and quick in this attire.

Ashoka also recalled that *Kalaripayattu* was very different from the *Dhanurvidya* he had learnt in Pataliputra in his past life. This made him even more curious to learn it.

When Ashoka began his lessons, he understood that learning *Kalaripayattu* begins not with aggression but with disciplining the body and mind.

Devi taught Ashoka, "The training starts with *Meithari* for disciplining the body and attaining mental balance. This first stage of training includes physical exercises to develop strength, flexibility, balance and stamina. It also includes jumps, low stances on the floor, circular movements and kicks. An attempt is made to understand and master different parts of the body. *Meithari* ensures alertness of the mind."

Devi was surprised that Ashoka could easily master *Meithari* in just nine days when it normally took months or even years for new students.

Ashoka mastered *Kolthari,* a self-defence method using a stick as a weapon, in the next nine days. This shocked Devi even more. She had not seen or heard of anyone mastering *Kolthari* so fast. In addition to being totally fearless and mentally alert, he also displayed amazing visual and hearing skills. She was forced to accept his mastery on the 9th day when he displayed his proficiency by fighting blindfolded many of the gurus of this Gurukul.

Devi was stunned when she saw that Ashoka needed no training in the metal weapons training *Angathari.* It was as though he was a natural fighter. This was till *Urumi* was handed to him.

The *Urumi* is a 5 foot long flexible metallic sword, which can be easily rolled to the hilt like a coil. It is referred to as *Chuttuval,* from the words for coiling or spinning (*chuttu*) and sword (*val*). Ashoka could just not get the knack of using it. He ended gashing himself every time he tried using it.

"The technique of using the *Urumi* was very different from fighting with the other weapons. It is a soft weapon in which the usage was accompanied by movements that were more like a dance. The centrifugal force generated by the movements of the fighter wielding it was adequate to inflict injury to the opponent or even multiple opponents. These movements had to be accompanied by agile body motions and spins," Devi demonstrated to Ashoka.

It took Ashoka three months of tireless practice before Devi would finally declare his mastery of the *Urumi*.

Finally, Ashoka was ready for *Verumkai* - the final training stage. This included the bare-hand fighting techniques of locking, gripping, throwing, blocking, striking and kicking techniques. This was mastered by Ashoka with great ease.

As a part of *Verumkai,* the *Marma Chikilsa* is a part taught to the most disciplined pupils who have mastered all other stages. It wasn't surprising that Devi decided to impart this knowledge to Ashoka. He was to be her ninth student to learn this last part of *Verumkai.*

She taught him how Shushruta the first known Surgeon of humanity had described the 107 *Marmas* or 'Seats of life' in a human body in his treatise on Surgery about 2500 years ago. Ashoka had also learnt about the

Marmas in *Padma Dham* when he had studied *Ayurveda* from Vaidya muni.

Thus began Ashoka's training on how he could cause a) immediate death b) a slow death c) immediate death on the removal of an inserted foreign body d) deformity to an opponent and e) severe pain. Devi noticed that Ashoka was able to master the techniques astonishingly quickly. She had taught him all the 36 methods known to her in just three days.

Once Devi told him that he had now completed his training and there was nothing more she could teach him, he suddenly seemed bewildered. Devi noticed that he had expected to learn more and assured him that she had taught him all that could be taught and she being the foremost Guru of *Kalaripayattu*, he had learnt everything.

The confused expression did not leave Ashoka for the next three minutes during which he blankly stared at her. When he was sure that Devi had taught all that she knew, he bowed down to Devi and then to Lord Parashuram and expressed his gratitude for having been taught *Kalaripayattu*. He paid her obeisance by lighting the lamp.

Suddenly, in a commanding voice, Ashoka told Devi, "It is time for you to learn the rest from me."

In the next 27 days, Ashoka feverishly taught Devi 71 techniques related the rest of 107 *Marmas* that Devi was not aware of.

Devi had been observing with great admiration as the pupil- turned-Guru overpoweringly taught her this forgotten knowledge. By the time this pupil turned Guru finished training Devi, she was sure that this person was a great warrior soul from the past and was now reborn in this form. She fell flat on her belly and paid her respects to Ashoka for teaching her the knowledge that had been lost in the ravages of time.

Ashoka spent the next six months teaching the pupils *Kalaripayattu* at Devi's Gurukul. He also learnt the science of *Kalari Marma* which used herbal oils application on the body followed by a foot massage. Ashoka learnt how this massage with herbal oils is applied based on the person's physical structure. He mastered the art of stimulating nerves and nerve points with herbal oils and with the pressure applied by the foot. This process ensured strengthening a warrior physically and mentally in order to face any kind of difficulties.

All along, Acharya and Ashoka also had been adding more students to the various Gurukuls they were setting up in the vicinity. About 9,000 villages had been covered in this region. Students who had been earlier taught by Acharya were now helping them set up new Gurukuls and in the spread of knowledge.

Ashoka and Acharya agreed that students in the Gurukuls should learn Martial arts like *Kalaripayattu*. They also knew that across the country there were more than 90 different forms of various martial arts. Hence, they agreed that each local martial art would be taught to the students of that region first. Once students had achieved mastery, they would have enough teachers to teach all these various forms across all the regions.

Ashoka now knew that the time had come to start moving northwards again. However, this time they would travel through the eastern part of the country instead of the western path they took when they had moved to the south.

Devi arranged a grand lunch to honour Ashoka before he left. All her present and former disciples came to attend the celebration. All members of Gurukul, including Acharya, were also present. Invitees also included family members of all those present. It was a grand event where Devi also presented an *Urumi* to Ashoka which he was to wear as a belt. At the end, Ashoka and Acharya approached Devi to thank her for this respect and love she had shown to both of them.

As they were about to leave, Devi introduced her granddaughter who had come from a long distance specifically to attend this felicitation. Devi kept talking at length about how her granddaughter Bhagirathi was an expert in *Kalaripayattu* and that Devi wanted her to take over the running of this Gurukul.

When she ended her discourse, Devi and Acharya suddenly noticed that both Ashoka and Bhagirathi were smiling knowingly at each other. It seemed as though they knew each other and that they shared some secret.

Devi was disappointed when Bhagirathi reiterated that she loved to travel and that she didn't want to be restricted to one place by teaching *Kalaripayattu.*

What Ashoka knew and understood and others did not was the fact that Bhagirathi was Rahu, one of the *Nava Grahas,* and she was involved in an ancient task that was of far greater importance to humanity.

The next morning Ashoka had the *Shiksha Stambha* erected at the Gurukul before they continued on their journey.

Dhauligiri

A shoka and Acharya reached Dhauli hills. On their way, they had come across the Chilika Lake.

Chilika Lake is the second largest lagoon on Earth and is a massive brackish water body of 1110 square kilometres. More than 180 species of migratory birds come here from the northern parts of the globe making it the largest winter habitat for these birds.

Ashoka and Acharya also got to know that this lake provided livelihood to about 180,000 people from 132 villages.

After going along the road, with banks of this lake on one side and with the Khallikote forest on the other side they came to the point where the river Daya culminated in this lake. They would move along the banks of Daya to reach their destination.

Ashoka's face had now turned pale with sorrow. He recalled with horror the scenes from the Kalinga war from his past life. This river and this land had been turned red with the blood of people of this land and along with that of horses and elephants.

As they approached the Dhauli hills, Ashoka saw the carving of an Elephant emerging from the rock. This was meant to be a representation of emergence of Gautama Buddha and it had stood there as a witness to the 2300 years gone by. He saw some of his messages from his earlier life that was conveyed directly to his people by these carvings on the rock. Nature had erased some of it. He recalled the entire message as he stood there reading the message written in *Brahmi*. Ashoka recalled that *Brahmi* was a type of *Prakrit* or natural writing and was one of the 18 scripts taught by the first Jain Tirthankara, Rishabanatha, to his daughter Brahmi.

On the Dhauli hills, he saw a white structure, the Pagoda. It had been rebuilt and his first thoughts were that this new structure should have been built in stone by Vishwakarma. Also, there was a recently made statue of Gautama Buddha in there.

At the foot of these hills was a Buddhist temple and also the Dhabaleshwar *Mandir*.

Ashoka and Acharya had to meet a *pujari* (priest) named Daksha at the Dhabaleshwar *Mandir*. Also, they would make a place near this *Mandir* their home for now.

The pujari took them to a school nearby. On the way to the school, the 70-year-old Daksha informed them that his daughter was one of the school teachers.

Once they reached the school, they were asked to wait for Daksha's daughter outside the classroom as she was teaching.

Ashoka looked inside the classroom and noticed the long braided hair of the teacher who was facing the blackboard. She seemed to be slightly over five feet in height. She was wearing a red saree with a white border. When she turned around, he could clearly see her round face with light brown skin and black eyes. He couldn't believe what his eyes had just seen. Just then the bell rang indicating the end of the class.

As she came out, the time had stopped for Ashoka. He felt as if a poem had just walked out of a book. The red sari now fully draped the dusk of her skin. The redness had a higher existence against the glistening of her dark eyes. Dark shiny hair gave way at the end before flowing down the curve of her back. Her simplicity carried an aura of substance and compassion.

When she came near them, Daksha introduced her to them. He addressed her as Kaurwaki while he introduced the visitors to her.

Acharya started conversing with her. Ashoka was speechlessly staring at Kaurwaki. She kept glancing at Ashoka as she spoke with Acharya.

Ashoka had still not recovered from the shock that fate had just played on him.

She was his Kaurwaki. She had the same name and very similar looks. Destiny had brought them together again after two millennia.

Kaurwaki

Ashoka's heart was fluttering with excitement and craved to meet Kaurwaki and having her beside him at all times.

Acharya had started the routine of teaching in the morning at Dhauli. Ashoka would start the day with his bath in the river Daya. He would then teach yoga for an hour at 6 am. Acharya would teach Sanskrit and the Vedas along with some forms of logic for the next two hours. All this would happen in a place next to the Dhabaleshwar Mandir and by the banks of the river Daya.

They would then have their breakfast in the temple.

Kaurwaki also started learning yoga and the Vedas by attending these morning gatherings.

Ashoka had decided that he would spend the next couple of hours in the school trying to understand what and how the children were being taught. It was more with an intention to stay close to Kaurwaki.

Ashoka could make out that despite being attracted to him, Kaurwaki had no idea about their being together in their earlier birth. He also had no intention of letting her know this.

It was about 30 days since Ashoka had set his eyes on Kaurwaki. Acharya, who had been constantly observing Ashoka, knew that the time was ripe.

Acharya reached out to Daksha with the proposal of Ashoka getting married to Kaurwaki. The *pujari* could not believe his ears and immediately agreed. He too had been witnessing the change in his daughter ever since the arrival of these two.

When the news reached Kaurwaki and Ashoka, it was like a dream come true for them. Both of them did not hesitate to show their excitement and immediately consented to this proposal.

Three days later they were married in Dhabaleshwar *Mandir*. Ashoka mentally prayed first to his parents and then to Gurudev as they could not be a part of this occasion. The ceremony then started with the recital of mantras and chants.

As part of the ritual, the bride and the groom had to circle the fire seven times signifying their commitment to each other not just in this life but for seven lives with *Agni* (God of Fire) as the witness. Ashoka couldn't help recalling all the previous six births where Kaurwaki, and he had been together as wife and husband. He knew he had fulfilled his commitment by marrying Kaurwaki for this seventh time.

Next six months were of marital bliss for the newlyweds with most time spent in the company of each other while continuing with their commitments for teaching.

Daksha knew a *tantric* named Bhairav who was a practitioner of the ancient science of *Tantra*. It was the custom in Daksha's family that a couple should learn *Tantra* and suggested it to them. Thus began Ashoka and Kaurwaki's initiation into the age-old knowledge of *Tantra* that revealed a deep understanding of the two opposing Masculine and Feminine Universal forces, the relationship of these two and eventually the inevitable reunion of these.

For this newly married couple madly in love with each other, spending their evenings together at the *tantrik's* place and learning the secrets of *Tantra* became one of the highlights in the six months that followed their marriage.

Chandaal

Ashoka was in his 39th year in 2043 CE. The Gurukuls had now covered more than 65,000 villages and towns. Each of these Gurukuls was now available for each village and town and also had multiple systems created by Chanakya and Vishwakarma for interconnectivity between these Gurukuls.

One aspect that was really bothering him now was that even though the majority of the people now had a greater level of knowledge and awareness, they were still not a part of the decision-making process in this democratic country.

Ashoka spoke about this concern in a special address to all people who were from these 65000 villages and towns. "People are used by politicians to only appropriate power with false promises. Very few of our genuine requirements are being taken care of as a part of the tokenism policy followed by our elected representatives. It has been the same ever since India had become a democracy. Only a small percentage of these representatives have truly worked for bettering the lives of the people and providing us with necessities."

"Many of the politicians have even used the divide and rule philosophy as a primary mode of gaining votes and keeping us, the people occupied in unnecessary issues. In four years from now, it would be a century of the rule of the people."

The unanimous opinion of all the people was that they should field their candidates in the coming elections, with Ashoka as their leader.

Ashoka was very reluctant initially as he wanted to concentrate on the next part of his plan in the task given by Gurudev. He recalled the trappings of power and would prefer to avoid it entirely. Also, it had been only six months since his marriage with Kaurwaki, and he wanted to spend as much time as possible with her.

However, the more he deliberated, the more he knew that this was the only choice left. This might even help hasten the mission given by Gurudev. However, this meant that he would spend lesser time with Kaurwaki.

Rather, reluctantly, he started formulating his strategy and selecting a team of probable representatives.

Even though Ashoka knew that this decision would ruffle many feathers, he was not prepared for the extent to which those in power would stoop to. As the news of this plan started spreading, the people who had seen the power of ruling over others started feeling insecure after understanding the strength this group wielded. They started using every trick in the world to ensure that this plan did not succeed. More and more incidents of intimidation, coaxing and divisive tactics were being reported.

However, Ashoka and the people chose to ignore these tactics used against them and kept on with their normal lives in addition to focusing on education and preparing themselves for the next elections.

With just less than nine months for the elections, time was running short and a lot needed to be accomplished. Ashoka and Kaurwaki got to spend less time together in the evenings post their *tantra* learning. Late evenings were now used as the meeting time for all exchange of election information and planning.

Just before sunset on one of those days, Ashoka and Kaurwaki had left Bhairav's place and were walking along the river Daya to get back to the Gurukul. Suddenly, a large group of men appeared out of nowhere and managed to bind Ashoka and Kaurwaki.

Ashoka, who had his mind preoccupied with the planning for elections, was very confused. By the time he recovered, he saw that he was being pinned down by four of these men. Kaurwaki was at about 50 meters distance from him and was being forcibly held by two others. Another 30 or 40 people stood between them.

The men threatened them the extreme consequence for having dared to think of participating in the elections.

His thoughts were racing now. He had tried so hard to avoid even the thoughts of violence from his past life. Now he was face to face with these barbarians in a situation he would have preferred to stay away from.

His thoughts were distracted by shrieks coming from Kaurwaki's direction. Now the two men who held her had knives pointed at her throat. Ashoka could not move and was being held back by the four people.

Suddenly Ashoka saw the two men slit her throat and let her limp body fall to the ground. He was shocked and speechless.

They had killed his Kaurwaki!

The men surrounding Ashoka were stunned by a loud shout which sounded more like a lion's roar to them and the four holding him back let go of their grip on him. Before they could realise what was happening, Ashoka was on his feet and was wildly swinging the *Urumi* that he had been wearing as a belt.

Hearing shouts, many from the Gurukul which was not very far-off had started rushing in this direction. When they reached this spot, they saw what was happening. They were stunned and stood like statues as they witnessed this horrifying sight.

In the blood-red light of the twilight, people saw Ashoka. He looked like a possessed man swinging his *Urumi* swiftly. Ashoka's moves resembled a well-choreographed dance. Yet he looked ferocious and the opponents were trying to stay clear of his swift assault. They could see bodies falling one after the other. Daksha and Bhairav, who were also witnessing this likened Ashoka's movements to the *Tandava* dance of Nataraja – the dance of the God of destruction.

At last, Ashoka reached the last two who had slit Kaurwaki's throat. His hands grabbed their necks, and he said something in their ears. Once they had vomited the names of the people who had sent them, their bodies also fell lifeless on to the ground.

People came nearer as Ashoka approached Kaurwaki's body. There were about 50 bodies lying around. When they examined the people lying limp on the ground, they were amazed to find not a single person had any slashes or injuries or external marks on their bodies. They were in fact breathing and had been rendered unconscious. It felt as though they had been paralysed.

Ashoka held the motionless body of Kaurwaki. He was devastated and wanted the people who had her killed punished.

Ashoka called Chanakya and briefed him on what had happened. He wanted two of Chanakya's birds. He gave Chanakya the specifications.

The moment Chanakya heard of Ashoka's plan, he was reluctant to agree as he disapproved of Ashoka's approach of revenge. However, Ashoka was adamant and managed to convince him. In less than 30 minutes, both the birds rested in Ashoka's hands.

Ashoka picked up the robotic birds and fed the names of those responsible for his dear wife's death into the memory of the robotic birds. Next, he fixed a range of coordinates as the possible locations where these people might be. At last, he placed one vial in each of the missile enclosures provided just before he set the birds free on their way to seek out the targets.

These birds had multiple recognition capabilities as required by Ashoka. In a short while, they had located, identified, reconfirmed and then shot the intended projectiles at their targets from close range. In less than three hours they were back and it was clear to Ashoka that the task was done.

Later, others got to know that these two were politicians who wanted Ashoka killed and had ended up killing Kaurwaki. They also had been rendered paralysed like the rest of the 50 who had attacked Ashoka. All attempts to get these 52 people out of their immobility were in vain. In fact, it was understood by the doctors treating them that all of them were reacting to all impulses like a normal conscious human being. However, they never could understand how to revive them. Ashoka had punished them with a living prison for what they had done.

When Bhagirathi and Devi heard about this, they knew that they could revive all these people immediately. However, both of them would not do so as they had heard the details of what had happened. They would also never attempt to interfere with the justice meted out by Ashoka.

Just after sunrise next morning and after everyone had paid their last respects, Kaurwaki's body was cremated.

Ashoka went into complete solitude for the next 10 days and came out after that to perform her final rituals.

Once all the rituals were done, everyone found Ashoka a changed man. He was more introspective, calm and composed most of the time. However, he had also become more affirmative and forceful in what he said. It looked like he was now in a hurry to finish the task assigned to him by Gurudev. His resolve to participate in the next elections had now become very firm, and he was leading from the front.

When news of how the 52 people had gone immobile reached all the people who were observing his rise as a political leader, they understood that Ashoka was clearly not a person who could be messed around with. However, the opponents used all opportunities to slander him for this act. They pulled out one name that had been used for the Mauryan Emperor Ashokavardhana in the past. They named him *Chandaal* which was a word negatively used for a cruel or an inhuman person. Ashoka, however, took it in his stride as he had done in his previous birth.

2044 Elections

Gurukuls had now expanded their operations to small towns after having covered most of the villages. People from all these villages and towns were brought under an umbrella organisation which was named the *Dharma Sansthapan Sanghathan* implying that it was an Organisation for the Establishment of *Dharma* or Righteousness. A triangular saffron flag with a rising sun at the centre came up atop the Gurukuls across the country. There were people in each Gurukul to coordinate activities and communicate across this strong network.

Acharya addressed the people during the formation of this *Sanghathan*. "*Dharma* is a way of living that is learnt from nature. The harmony seen in the universe is a result of *Dharma*. Living beings have to learn to live in synchronisation with the nature by learning from our universe. This is possible by performing certain duties, exercising certain rights and following nature's laws. Ensuring this right way of living requires a certain conduct along with some qualities to be followed," he said.

The groundwork to form the political party had been done. The entry of *Dharma Sansthapan* Party into the electoral battle was greeted with unprecedented enthusiasm across the country. The rising sun gave hope of a new vibrant Bhaaratha. Other parties were in awe of the swiftness and efficiency with which the party established its overwhelming presence across the nation. Within seven days of the announcement of the name of the party, the unit was election-ready.

Then it was time for Ashoka, Acharya, Chanakya and Vishwakarma to go to Nashik *Kumbha Mela* to seek the blessings of Gurudev. The smile with which Gurudev greeted them spoke a million words.

On the day of the elections, everyone was present in their own constituencies to cast their vote. Ashoka had arrived in Chunar a day before the elections. The festive spirit among the people brought a smile to his face.

The next few days were spent in meditation and rest by Ashoka. His body begged for mercy. He had been crisscrossing the country to demonstrate that he was leading from the front. The results of the elections would take another couple of days. Soon, he would be joined by Chanakya, and then they would proceed to Delhi.

On the morning of the results, Ashoka finished his meditation and joined Chanakya for breakfast. They ate in silence. Chanakya watched Ashoka's calm effect and wondered how someone could be so detached. "The Buddha would be proud of this man," thought Chanakya.

During the first hour of the counting of votes, leaders from various political parties came on various channels and made tall claims. Two hours later, there was disbelief writ large on their faces. By noon, none of these leaders was available for comments. The demolition had been completed. Ordinary people from villages and small towns had decided they needed a change. BBC and CNN reported that an electoral coup had taken place in India, stealthily and silently.

Maiden Parliament Address

Ashoka threw a glance around the Central Hall of the Parliament and saw 72% of the seats being occupied by MP's from his party. Sixty per cent of these were women.

He got up to deliver his maiden address to this house. He closed his eyes to first pray to Gurudev and then to his parents.

Before he could even finish his prayers, he started hearing a voice from the opposite side. However, he continued and finished his prayers.

When he opened his eyes, he saw the face from which this voice was continuing to emerge. The impatient man was blabbering something loudly about how a large group of people ignorant about the traditions of the House had landed here. This voice was clearly showing arrogance and disdain.

He recognised the face as that of a fifth-generation politician in the family that had haughtily ruled the country instead of being the representatives of people they were meant to be. They had broken every law that had been formed and were known to look down on those who had voted for them.

As he continued his mocking, there was continuous sneering from his fellows, who seemed very pleased to do any of his biddings.

All the while, Ashoka kept staring calmly at him. Soon, Ashoka's eyes started turning red, but the face maintained composure.

As Ashoka's eyes started appearing redder, the voice from the opposite side slowly changed to a whimper. However, Ashoka continued to stare with a calm face. Suddenly, without any warning, the whimper changed to loud and shrill gibberish. Very soon, this politician had to be lifted out of the Parliament. Later, it was found that he had gone completely insane and had to be moved permanently to a mental asylum.

After he had been taken out, there was a lull as Ashoka started looking around as if for permission to speak. None of those present on the opposite side wanted to look into his eyes and tried to look down.

Then Ashoka started his address.

"I would prefer to speak in Sanskrit. It is not because I know that the majority in the house knows this language or that the people they represented are conversant with this language."

Ashoka went on to explain how this language could easily express what was spoken while giving very less room for misinterpretations. He also gave multiple examples of the richness of Sanskrit. Ashoka showed how different words could be used to get slightly different meanings. He showed how foreign and some vernacular languages had blended these different shades into one word and could easily misrepresent what was said and even change the meaning behind what was said.

Ashoka suggested, "All the proceedings, laws, etc. should use this language. All those who are not familiar with this language can easily use the auto-translators available at their seats or gradually learn it."

Since no one had any objections to this suggestion, he started speaking in Sanskrit.

He first thanked the people for giving all those present in this house an opportunity to represent the people.

Ashoka then expressed concern over the way the representatives had let down the very people who voted for them and how the various Pillars of Democracy had been misused by a very few who were mandated to perform some functions.

"In some cases, it was worse than the rule of the barbaric rulers of the past," Askoka continued. He was deeply anguished that this form of democracy did not truly reflect 'The Rule of the People.'

"I am clear that this has to change. However, I also admit that this cannot happen overnight and it had to be done step by step. Wherever demolition of the parts of system and rebuilding is necessary, it has to be done. My understanding is that the laws, institutions, principles and all the arms of this democratic system are for binding the people together as a unit which formed this nation. They were clearly not meant to bind them in chains. These are a means to give the people a common identity while understanding, appreciating and allowing their uniqueness to flourish."

He went on to add how, for the very first time, a majority of the people of this nation had reached a very high level of awareness in a very short time, how this had clearly changed from the recent past and also how it had reflected in their representation in this House. He felt that it was time to bring the rest of the people to this level of awareness.

Next, he started speaking of the various excesses that had happened over the past millennium and how it had changed the outlook of *Bhaarata* from a Golden Era to the era of hoarding. The Barbarians' age was followed by people who wanted resources for their machines and ended up even transforming humans into machines. "They also changed the education system to meet these objectives. This was eventually followed by the age of Energy Blackmail and of the Misinformation Era. Money and Might were the two primary objectives of those people who perpetuated the excesses. There were no morals followed by these people. The excesses were possible because the people who were given responsibility were trusted or seen to be more powerful. Hence, the majority of people had considered that they were weak, or they simply practised ignorance and allowed these excesses to go unabated. It is our responsibility to ensure that people remain as a Unified Force to decide the destiny of this nation. This strength should be used to counter any attempts at unrestrained behaviour in the future."

"All attempts made to divide people have to be demolished one at a time. As a first step, I suggest that *Bhaarata* is divided only based on the geographical locations into 9 parts i.e. North, South, East, West, North-east and the Central part which would have three regions. All the Islands could form the ninth region."

"Money and Might in this Rule of People should jointly and equally belong to the very same people and should not be the privilege of a few," Ashoka continued.

Ashoka talked about the *Dharma Chakra* or the Wheel of Dharma.

"The *Dharma Chakra* has twenty-four spokes. I suggest that an equal number of people from the following 24 categories be the ones who would represent the people if we are to establish true People's representation."

The 24 spokes according to Ashoka were aligned to the following:

1. Respect for all beings & Nature

2. Land

3. Water

4. Food providers

5. Textiles and other wearable items

6. Craftsmen

7. Health of Humans and other life forms

8. Energy

9. Teaching

10. Security

11. External Affairs

12. Art, Culture, Mythology and Entertainment

13. Sports and Physical activities

14. Ancient Sciences, Modern Sciences, Communication

15. Transportation and related Infrastructure

16. Builders, Designers and Planners

17. Manufacturing

18. Traders and other service providers

19. Financial Matters

20. Elections Monitoring and Control

21. Administration

22. Legislature

23. Judiciary

24. Astronomy & Space Exploration

"It is up to this house to decide if other professions need to be added to these twenty-four categories.

This categorisation should be the basis of representation of people, and these categories will form the 'Spokes of the Democratic Wheel' that will drive our democracy."

"The Grand Council which would be created by these members will be the voice of the people. People who have elected the members should be able to change these representatives as and when required even if their assigned terms are not completed. The Grand Council would need to take the approval of the people on all decisions. There should be no scope for any centralisation of power. Technology, as well as the people's willingness, had ensured that people can and will take decisions faster."

"All 24 of these categories will have their separate individual council which will be made up of representatives in their individual categories."

"For any specific matter which might be beyond their expertise, they could appoint a smaller and specific council that would appropriately provide guidance on those particular matters."

"There are many institutions related to each of these 24 categories with government employed people working in them. These employees should also be given short and fixed terms. Their performance shall be monitored by the respective category council members, in addition to ensuring their smooth functioning of the institutions. For example, the Judiciary's functioning will be monitored by the representatives of the judicial council. However, if for any reason the majority of people so decide, they could ensure that these employees are also called back from their respective roles."

Ashoka continued, "We also have to ensure that all the remnants of the past excesses shall be equally available to all the people."

"We request all people concerned to willingly return to the people the wealth illegally snatched in the past, failing which, they shall be forced by the law of the people to do so."

By now the people sitting on the opposite side were beginning to sweat. The heat that had been turned on by Ashoka's words, coupled with the absence of their leader, was turning into a nightmare come true for them. However, not one word came out of anyone's mouth. They didn't realise that this was just the beginning. Their eyes now started to wander looking into each other's eyes for solace.

When they were sure that none of them would utter a word, they started looking in the direction of the 72% who were from Ashoka's party.

The representatives of the majority were absorbing every detail of what was being said. To the minority in this house, this majority group seemed even meeker and that they were also sheepishly accepting what their leader had said. They didn't realise that if Ashoka was a lion, then this group backing him was that of tigers. They had been trained and would eventually dissect and analyse all aspects of everything Ashoka had said before ensuring that it would be passed on to the people they represented. These representatives had a duty to fulfill to the people who had voted them as well as the nation they belonged to and not sheepishly accept what was said even if they knew it was right. They were the living examples of the ancient and time tested logic and morality.

Elixir of Life

Ashoka had learnt about how the ancient Indians understood water and hydrology so well. In fact, they had a very deep understanding of the hydrologic cycle which involved evaporation, condensation, precipitation as rainfall or snowfall. There are multiple references of this understanding in all ancient texts, including the various Vedic literature, *Puranas, Mayurachaitraka, Arthashastra, Meghamala*, Jain and Buddhist literature. Even a poem like *Meghadhoota* of Kalidasa displayed some of this understanding.

One more such example from the past was that of Varahamihira. He was a 6th Century mathematician and teacher who had influenced a lot of people during his time and even much later. His teachings were widely regarded by locals and foreigners as one of the best for many centuries that followed. *Brihat Samhita* or a Great Compilation is one such text which covers a wide variety of topics. Varahamihira also discussed hydrology in great detail in *Brihat Samhita*.

All along the known history to the present time, there was a good understanding of water. However, there were multiple instances across these times on how there was a flood or a famine, some of which had even changed the course of history. This situation had continued to the present day. In the past, the reasons for this may have been varied. However, in the present day, it was purely due to the apathy of the authorities concerned.

Ashoka knew this had to change. Gurukuls had developed their ingenious ways to tackle this problem locally. Now with three years left for the 100th anniversary of Independence, Ashoka made up his mind that all life in this country should never be deprived of water at any time.

He summoned various experts, and suggestions were taken on how to address this issue. All the learning from across the country, as well as the world was taken.

First, every known technology was used to remap every inch and every contour of the land. The altitudes at each of these locations were mapped very carefully.

Simultaneously, all the water sources were mapped. This included all rivers, reservoirs, lakes, ponds, wells and geysers. They also mapped every known aquifer under the ground.

Additionally, every primary source of the above sources was also mapped along with their interconnections. This included the seasonal rains and the glaciers which formed the sources of some rivers.

Once various consumers used the water, this wastewater would be treated and reused by sending it to its source. Sometimes it would be even untreated and might end up in separate rivulets and finally end in the ground or end up in the larger sources of water like lakes, rivers or the sea. The understanding of the quality of all of this water in addition to that of its sources was very important. This was more important as the contaminants left over from the human excesses of the past had contaminated all aspects of nature. Additionally, there were other naturally occurring undesirables that had to be removed before it reached the people.

Atmospheric conditions, including temperature, pressure and wind cycles, had to be understood. Patterns of local weather and the broader climate would also have to be mapped.

Finally, a thorough understanding of humidity levels of the air was also made. Air had started becoming a source of water in many areas.

Within 90 days, blueprints were drawn and plans were made. The plan was to ensure that water of the required quality reaches every inch of the land. Every source of water would be connected across the country like the veins of a leaf to meet this end.

The action started across all the regions instantaneously.

New tributaries, rivulets, canals and channels started connecting all the water sources from perennial rivers to the consumers. Enough storage of water above the ground and below the ground was ensured to take care of any contingencies. To meet this objective, there were paths created across hills and mountains in some places. Even underground channels were created at many places to ensure a smooth and gradual gravitational flow of water.

Water was monitored continuously for quantity and quality and was treated to ensure its suitability for the desired use. To ensure this, all villages, towns and cities now had monitoring stations which used Chankya's birds as well as Vishwakarma's innovative continuous monitoring devices.

This regular monitoring ensured the directions in which the treated water would flow. It was ensured that water could move in any direction based on the need.

All natural forms of energy, like solar energy, wind energy and hydro energy, had been used to ensure that water moves against the gravity of the earth through newly created channels and pipes. Experiments were also made to evaporate massive amounts of treated water from the seas and transport it through pipelines against gravity or use the natural drift of air to transport this water vapour.

If there was a shortage at any place, treated water from the seas, on either side would be used to replenish the shortage by transporting it to those areas.

The pathways and the reservoirs were so designed to prevent any flooding.

All these efforts were made possible by the dedicated actions of the people who formed the 'Water Spoke' of this democratic setup.

It took nine years of dedicated efforts and measures to achieve this mammoth task. When the task was finally finished, it ensured that every form of life would never be deprived of this *Elixir of Life*.

Vishwa Vidyalayas

A shoka summoned the *Nava Grahas*. They appeared in the same order as they always did.

His message to each one of them was the same. They were to be involved in setting up of 729 *Vishwa Vidyalayas* or Centres of Higher Learning. These would be spread across the nine regions and each region would have 81 *Vishwa Vidyalayas*.

Each of the *Nava Grahas* had to select 81 people who would, in turn, pick up a subject of their expertise and mentor the *Acharyas* or teachers at these places. This meant that each of 729 experts would have to mentor at one of these 729 *Vishwa Vidyalayas*.

"It is of great importance to ensure that people quickly learn and develop the understanding that will help bridge the gap between the ancient and modern sciences. This knowledge that the students will acquire from these *Vishwa Vidyalayas* should produce things that would be useful to the people in their everyday life," said Ashoka.

"Additionally, students must learn from the way nature has developed and get inspired from it to develop new tools for people's use and convenience."

"At the same time, the new developments should help preserve nature and should not harm it or destroy it as has happened in the recent past."

In the nine years that followed, people had started experiencing or utilising the fruits of this initiative. A huge wave of a different type of knowledge was spreading across the country.

One of the 729 *Vishwa Vidyalayas* had created solutions that now ensured that energy could be easily generated in multiple ways by using natural forces. Energy was available freely to everyone.

Another *Vishwa Vidyalaya* started developing medicines along with treatments for ailments using a holistic approach.

A third *Vishwa Vidyalaya* was redefining air transportation. *Vimanas* of the past were now becoming a reality. Not just that, they were moving beyond with a greater understanding using these for outer space exploration.

Nature below the sea had a lot to share in terms of the wealth of knowledge available at those depths. It had remained largely unexplored as the conditions were harsh and the technology available earlier could not withstand the pressures of tens of thousands of feet of water at its depths. All that changed the moment one of the *Vishwa Vidyalayas* developed materials from the new understanding of how things worked at the smallest scale of the molecules and how this could be innovatively used to create materials which could be used in the harshest of conditions.

Plastics and other polymer wastes were one of the lingering reminders of past ignorance. Different strains of artificial microbes which would ingest these polymers to meet their energy requirements and create wastes which could be used by nature easily were developed. Each of the different strains of microbes would be released into the atmosphere. They would identify the type of polymer they were meant to consume and then start ingesting it. They would also replicate to form large colonies at the source of their food. However, once their food supply - which was a particular type of polymer - was not available, they would die as these strains could not use any other type of food. It took about 9 years for almost all the polymer wastes to be eliminated. 2060 was declared the year in which Earth would be rid of all polymer wastes from the land and from the water.

These 729 *Vishwa Vidyalayas* were to surpass the great *Vishwa Vidyalayas* of the past and the best modern universities in all respects.

Ashoka was pleased that this was the best tribute that one could pay to the *Vishwa Vidyalayas* of Takshashila, Nalanda, Vikramashila, Pusphagiri, Vallabhi, Somapura, Odantapuri and the many other great *Vishwa Vidyalayas* of the past, which had been destroyed by barbarians.

Hell on Earth

Ashoka knew that there has to be a very strong deterrent which would prevent either the citizens of *Bhaarata* or foreigners from trying to destroy or even think of destroying the unity of the people.

History had taught that barbarians, usurpers and hoarders understand only one language. A special place would have to be created that would be a living hell for anyone considered so by a majority of the people.

He consulted with a host of people, and finally, plans were ready for this 'Hell on Earth'.

One uninhabited island was chosen for this hell. The location of this was not made known to anyone except a few in the law enforcement.

It was inspired based on the ancient war technique of "*Chakravyuha*" or "*Padmavyuha*".

Chakra means a disc or a circle or a ring and *Vyuha* means formation.

Chakravyuha was a formation of warriors in seven concentric spirals. These spirals would continuously move with the aim of confusing and eventually defeating a formidable enemy. It was also used to protect important people in the wars.

The *Chakravyuha* was difficult to penetrate as the person attempting would be confused and would be unable to focus on a still target in front, as the targets keep changing with the rotation of these rings.

If at all an attacker was able to penetrate one ring and get inside the *Chakravyuha*, the rotating nature of this *Vyuha* made sure that the ring he had penetrated closed behind him quickly. This would ensure that the attacker got trapped within the *Chakravyuha*.

In short, a *Chakravyuha* must be a multi-layered circular labyrinthine maze in which weak and strong warriors were strategically placed, and each of the layers is presented with possible openings that were closely guarded by one of the strongest warriors and his group of warriors.

The *Chakravyuha* formation was never visible to the enemy from the ground. This meant that it had to be used only in battles which were fought on the plain ground with the enemy having no way of observing from a higher altitude.

This hell inspired by *Chakravyuha* was completed with various illusions that would attract the prisoner in a particular direction.

When a prisoner was left on this island, he would see this island end to end with some trees on it and the ocean surrounding it. In fact, it would look like a paradise.

However, once the prisoner went anywhere close to the trees or tried to get into the water, the illusions would begin.

Mirrors would suddenly appear to surround the prisoner in all directions; the temperature would change drastically. Suddenly, there would be darkness or a huge flood of blinding lights which would be of different colours.

Sinkholes would appear suddenly on the ground taking him into a limitless fall and then eject him out of this hole without warning.

The sounds that would be created were so strange that they would drive any person insane.

Each of these labyrinths would torture a person enough till he is directed into the next labyrinth.

The prisoner, however, would be kept alive by ensuring that he ate some food and drank some water.

It was estimated that most people would break down in three days of stay here and the toughest could survive for a maximum of seven days in this hell.

However, this was to be used only in the rarest of rare cases. Hence, enough publicity was given about this 'Living Hell'. This ensured that even the toughest criminals gave up their criminal ways due to the fear of entering this 'Hell on Earth'.

A Neighbour's Misadventure

Twelve years had passed since the 2044 elections. Acharya's *Gurukuls* now covered every inch of the land. This also meant that the subsequent elections of 2049 and 2054 brought greater majority and more representatives of Ashoka's party to the various public positions.

Every election brought in fresh representatives as people felt that other citizens should get a chance to use their skills for the country. This also meant that there would be freshness in the perspective brought in by the newly elected representatives. However, everyone wanted Ashoka to continue to lead, and he continued as a common thread that connected the people and their representatives.

One by one, the new spokes of the democratic set up were shaping up as had been envisaged by Ashoka. People were beginning to see a Golden Age emerging on the horizon. However, a lot needed to be done to make sure that they as well as the future generations lived in the Golden Age.

This progress was not palatable to many. This included some from outside who had thrived financially by trying to create instability in this country. Their supporters within India had dwindled to a point of extinction.

Rizwan Pasha was one such person who was a part of the Pakistani armed forces. Rizwan had more than one reason to feel jealous and helpless. However, he knew all of this would change now as the final piece of his master plan fell into place.

Rizwan Pasha was now staring at the screens as he sat in the Military Command Centre. Everything had gone precisely as per the plan and these final moments were making him nervous with excitement. He could feel his palms sweat as he watched the part of the screen which displayed the countdown timers. His short pointed hair seemed to be firmly standing with military discipline. His longish face and his eyes with dark circles around them expressed nothing of the elation he was experiencing. Only his nose gave away his crookedness.

'Coward of Pakistan' was the nickname General Rizwan Pasha had earned. He had managed to take this mockery in his stride and always bid for his time. He was sure it would come slowly but surely. Rizwan had played his pawns carefully one at a time, at the same time remaining in the background always, allowing foolish people take credit for his successes all the while and being the fallback guy when things went wrong. He was also clear in his mind that he would never ever volunteer to be in the front of any military action and end up like other distinguished military members of his family.

Rizwan had always carefully chosen a mentor among his superiors as well as the politicians and made sure he would be at their beck and call. His present mentor was a 4th generation political leader who considered him an extremely loyal dog. This had finally ensured that he and only he would be chosen as the Joint Chief of Armed Forces over all other contenders, all of who were senior to him in age and experience.

Rizwan came from a financially poor family like most military men. It was common knowledge that the financially underprivileged were always the cannon fodder in a military force like that of Pakistan.

Rizwan's family had lived in Hyderabad till they were forced to move to Pakistan during the Partition with India. Rizwan's was the fourth generation after that. This large Pasha family, comprising 200 members who had started from *Nizam's* Hyderabad, was reduced to 120 by the time they crossed over to the newly formed Pakistan. The horrors and hardships the family had endured made sure many generations to come would continue to hate India.

His great-grandfather Syed Pasha had volunteered to join the Pakistan army immediately on arriving in Pakistan. He was never heard of again and most probably got killed as soon as he was in the line of Indian fire in his country's first misadventure in Kashmir.

His grandfathers Mohammed Pasha and Salim Pasha were the next to be part of the military.

Mohammed Pasha joined the elite Ghajnavi force of the legendary Major Malik Munawar Khan Awan in 1965. He was among the few who died while trying to capture the Munawar Pass.

Salim Pasha had led the 42 tanks in the Battle of Longewal six years later in 1971 and advanced deep into the enemy territory in the dark of the night. This was one of the most dim-witted military plans and the very next day they had become sitting ducks to the Indian Air fire. Rizwan had heard his grandfather's cry for help probably just before he was killed, on a radio recorded message, many decades later.

Salman Pasha, his uncle was a part of the battalion which had captured and occupied Point 4875 of Mushkoh Valley in the 1999 Kargil War. When his dead body arrived, it was found to have been punctured completely with AK-47 bullets. One of the snipers who accompanied the body had assured the family that the enemy who did this to his friend and colleague Salman had been shot and killed by him. Rizwan was less than a year old at that time.

Rizwan's thoughts came back to the present as he glanced at the screens. He was now 58 old and the years of long-suffering and wait would soon come to an end.

He smiled as he recalled the day before this month of Ramadan had begun. Rizwan had been summoned to the Prime Minister's office and informed of the decision to make him the Joint Chief of Armed forces. The very next day, which was the first day of this holy month, he had assumed charge as the Joint Chief. He had taken this as a good omen; a sign from God to execute his plan.

General Rizwan Pasha visited as many military installations as was physically possible in the last three weeks, especially while observing the rigor of fasting in this holy month. For any outsider, it looked like a newly appointed Joint Chief taking stock of the situation under his command. However, his idea was to quickly execute his plan and ensure total enemy destruction before the end of this holy month. He was ensuring that all pieces of his plan fell properly in place.

Rizwan had spent a great part of the time trying to make sure that the plan is executed without any flaws. A lot of detailing and effort had gone into synchronising the efforts to ensure that perfection to the very last microsecond would be achieved. To ensure synchronicity, Global Positioning Satellites (GPS) receivers would be used in all command centers. This would compute a solution that simultaneously provided Position and Time (P&T).

By using the timestamps transmitted by the satellites in this solution, precision in time synchronisation would be achieved at the microsecond level.

His eyes now moved to the large 3D projection in the middle of the room. The Pakistan map, with all its amazing natural coloured terrains, was clearly visible to all the 200 people in this room.

He looked at the sky through the large window. The sky, however, was not clear. In fact, it was overcast with heavy dark clouds, and it had just started raining. It looked as though there would be torrential rains anytime now. Information had come in that the weather was similar at all other military installations. He was not letting these gloomy clouds dampen his spirits or make any changes to his plans which were now in the last phase of execution.

His attention turned back to the 3D projection in the centre and then more specifically to the 300 red lights flickering on the map. On his signal, they turned orange.

Chants of 'God is great' were heard in the room followed by pin drop silence.

A shiver ran through Rizwan's spine and his body trembled as he now had to give the final nod.

All 300 Nuclear warheads available had been fitted on to the surface missiles and were now ready to be launched.

Initially, Rizwan had apprehensions about the efficacy of this plan as many of these warheads were antique.

Qadar Khan, who headed the Nuclear Defence Program, had shown how these warheads were painstakingly maintained. "Their upkeep is the key to the Pakistani Atomic Deterrence Program." Qadar Khan had said.

300 Missiles with nuclear warheads were now aimed at 300 Indian cities, towns and military installations. India would be annihilated even before they have a chance to strike back. He couldn't imagine a better revenge on the Indians for what the country had done to his 84 family members and to the many other Pakistanis who had given their lives for their beloved country. This would also be a befitting reply for all the insulting defeats his beloved country, Pakistan, had suffered at the hands of India ever since they were separated into different nations.

General Rizwan Pasha knew that he would no longer be called the 'Coward of Pakistan'. He would now be compared with the greatest. He liked the title 'Quaid-e-Azam'. A wry smile escaped him as his eyes narrowed to focus on the flickering lights.

The atmosphere in the room at the Military Command Centre suddenly turned electric as all the 300 flickering lights turned green and stopped flickering on his authorisation.

The countdown had started 10, 9, 8, ...

Curse of Indus Valley

The 200 pairs of eyes at the Military Command Centre turned their heads with military precision to see outside through the towering transparent window as the countdown ended. They saw the liftoff of the most potent ICBM Shaheen X, which had been just launched from about 100 meters away.

Once the awe of the missile take-off was digested, the smiles on all the faces started appearing. As they were about to start clapping, they first saw a blinding light which made them turn their heads away in a reflex action. This was followed by a sonic boom and the last thing they heard was the crashing of the window.

The seismographs across the Earth detected multiple waves originating from Pakistan.

The 300 missiles launched simultaneously had met a similar fate or had failed to take off. There were multiple nuclear blasts within a few milliseconds after liftoff. There were blasts even in some missiles that had failed to lift off. All blasts were seemingly triggered by premature detonations.

In a few minutes, all top global government leaders were looking to receive the live feed of the dreadful destruction from their satellites in space. Although these satellites could not help observation in the visible light range using the normal cameras owing to the heavy clouds, the infrared (IR) cameras helped to overcome this drawback and passed on the necessary inputs.

The thermal radiation along with the gamma, neutron radiation and the ionising after effects of the nuclear radiation had ensured total destruction. The dark clouds had poured down and hammered such heavy rains that it drenched Pakistan like never before. No typical mushroom clouds had formed from any of these blasts. It was as if the smoke and the nuclear material had been sent back to the ground and absorbed into the Pakistani soil almost as soon as it had formed. However, the damage and destruction was done all around the blast sites which covered most of Pakistan.

Pakistan had been annihilated in the worst known human-created disaster ever.

Bizarre theories started appearing about the cause of this catastrophe.

Many attributed this to the 'Curse of Indus Valley' as stories were told likening this disaster to a similar destruction in the past which had destroyed an ancient civilisation.

Some thought India had carried out a nuclear attack on Pakistan which was quickly denied by India.

It was confirmed that 300 missiles of Pakistani origin had taken off from different parts of that country. This made some to conclude that an anti-missile swarm of Chanakya's insect drones had detonated the missiles immediately post-liftoff.

Others believed that the Strategic Defence Initiative (SDI) or more commonly known as the Star Wars programme of the consortium of some countries had triggered premature nuclear explosions of the warheads immediately post the take off of these missiles.

Then there were conspiracy theories of guardian aliens who had destroyed the nuclear weapons to prevent an all-out nuclear war on Earth.

Across the globe, the seismic aftershocks were now slowly increasing in intensity.

The Day The Earth Really Shook

Chanakya, who was now the head of the Intelligence and Counter Measures, interrupted the Prime Minister's meeting with 100 administrators in the large meeting room and informed Ashoka of the Pakistan disaster. He directed that everyone should immediately enter the nuclear shelter.

Instructions were also passed to the entire administration, and they were now directed to enter the underground fortress built 30 meters below the ground specifically to protect from a nuclear attack or any other disaster.

On the way to the subterranean facility, Chanakya whispered to Ashoka, "The Phase-1 of the counter to Pakistani attack had gone precisely as planned. It is now time for the Phase-2 of the plan to be set into motion." However, he again cautioned Ashoka, as he had done during the planning phase that many forces of nature could now come into play and might be beyond any of countermeasures already in place.

The underground shelter was fully functional in less than 15 minutes with all important people entering this underground city through various tunnels.

All across India, a similar exercise was undertaken with all city and town management moving into their respective shelters.

The visuals of the disaster zones in Pakistan were being relayed live. There had been an extremely heavy downpour all across the Pakistan blast sites immediately after the blasts. This kept interrupting the live feed. Seismograph feeds were showing the changing intensity of the waves of this ground shaking event. These ripples could be felt all across India and other neighbouring countries.

Ashoka directed Chanakya to activate all his robotic birds, insects and eyes across the country. Next, he started addressing the National Disaster Management Group, Armed Forces, Administration and Volunteer Organisations to start the drills and be on standby for any eventuality. He also wanted information to be circulated across the country.

Disaster Management had swiftly conveyed to all people to move out of buildings. The military command base conveyed that their drills had started, and they were on standby. People at sea were given evacuation orders to prevent any mishaps in case of any tsunamis. All nuclear reactors were shut down. Fortunately, water in all dams was less than 40 percent. However, their administrators were asked to be on high alert.

The aftershocks were being felt at regular intervals of 7 to 10 minutes, and these showed a trend of increasing intensity.

Acharya was in Ujjain and had started observing ants coming out of the ground. All animals had suddenly become very restless. Insects and birds were seen flying frantically. Nature was signalling uncertainty. He immediately had all the students move in all directions and inform all around the Gurukul to move to open spaces. Next, he connected with all Gurukuls to check if they were observing anything similar. After they had confirmed his observations, he wanted everyone to make sure that people were moved out into the open.

About one hour after the Pakistan catastrophe, a sudden and massive shockwave was felt. This was like no other in its intensity. The seismographs recorded a peak intensity of 9.9 on the Richter scale. It was the most intense earthquake in recorded history. It was worse than any other known earthquake as the epicentre was not one but multiple. This earthquake was felt not just in India and Pakistan, but also all in other countries around them.

People could see large buildings shake before they fell. Smaller ones were crumbling. Bridges were falling. Cracks had started appearing in the ground and in some places people saw with awe the opening of the ground which seemed to come towards them or moving away from them like a snake. Trees were shaking and palm trees swinging widely.

After a few minutes, when all the aftershocks had subsided, people started to understand the impact of this. Most of the buildings were razed to the ground and about 30% of the buildings which looked intact would be later found to have been compromised structurally.

Even the rivers had changed their course. Hot water and steam jets were being spewed from openings on the surface of the earth.

The intensity of the earthquake could also be clearly felt even in the underground shelters. However, there was no damage to any of these. As the gravity of the situation was being assessed, Ashoka directed the emergency response teams and military who were on standby to begin rescue operations immediately.

The worst nightmare had come true. It took two weeks to estimate the loss of lives. At the last count, it was estimated that 15% of the human population was no more! The condition was similar in all countries affected by this earthquake.

A tsunami followed from south of Afghanistan moving in all directions in the Arabian Sea. There was a similar tsunami to the east of India that travelled into the Bay of Bengal. Islands and coastal regions in the path of both these tsunamis were inundated and destroyed.

The next four weeks saw people struggling to come to terms with the disaster and damage around them. The greatest losses to life and property were in the cities. Towns had lesser damage, and villages were the least affected.

Across cities and towns, the familiar skylines of manmade structures had now disappeared. Nature had now reclaimed its place.

Cremation grounds were working overtime with mass cremations. Ashoka directed that the solar-powered mass cremation facilities be quickly increased multi-fold as not many human burials could be accommodated and all the dead bodies would have to be cremated. There were also other animals' bodies which had to be quickly disposed of.

Acharya's disciples across the country worked with the military, administration and social organisations to create temporary shelters. Food and water supply were quickly restored within a few days.

Ashoka had instructed Vishwakarma to ensure that the damaged buildings and structures were quickly brought down using sonic cannons. This ensured quicker demolition and rapid clearance of the rubble. Metals used in the structures were the toughest to handle and these were slowly being transported to large temporary scrap yards.

By the time the intensity of this disaster was fully understood, it had been found that the Indian peninsular plate had separated from the Eurasian Plate and moved south by about 30 metres. Starting from the Arabian Sea in the west to Bay of Bengal in the east, a new ridge had formed between the Eurasian plate and the Indian plate uniting the waters from these seas.

This ridge moved along the Chaman fault and the Sulaiman Range in the west along the Main Pamir Thrust which is north of the Hindu Kush Mountains, moving down eastwards along the Karakorum Thrust and the Indus-Tsangpo Suture to the south of Tibetan Plateau and finally moving south along Sagaing fault in the east.

The height of the Himalayas in the north had reduced by about 90 meters which resulted in the moving up of the southern Part of the Indian plate and bringing a part of the submerged and long-lost Kumari Kandam above the sea level. The eastern and western coastlines saw increase in land giving the impression that the seas had receded farther away.

A few weeks later, water had started flowing in India along the path of a long-lost ancient river – Saraswati. This river was no longer considered mythical or confined only to the Vedic texts. It had again come alive and would eventually be the largest of the rivers. In due course, Saraswati would convert the deserts in its path to the most fertile lands and would help regain their past glory. In this land, Saraswati was not just a river but also the Goddess of learning. The interconnections of rivers meant that the waters of Saraswati would now touch every part of the land. It would now be a part of all the veins of the water network. People of this land had always believed that *Vidya* or the right knowledge was enough for Saraswati or the Goddess of learning to appear. They were to be proven wrong soon. Much more was required for Saraswati to continue to stay. *Avidya* which meant ignorance or incorrect knowledge was also to be removed.

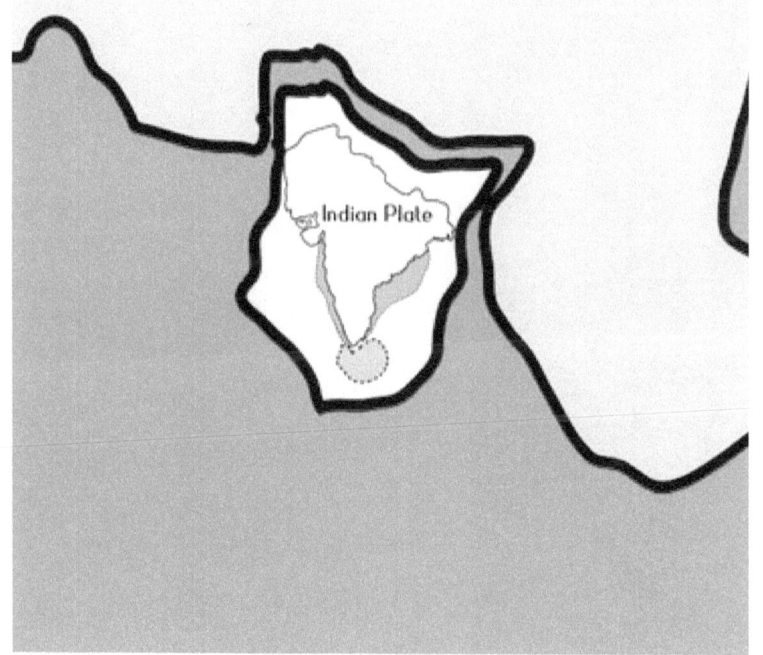

The Last Sacrifice

Very few facilities across the country had underground shelters. These were used either by the administration, the military, sensitive establishments or the research labs. Most of these underground structures had survived the tremors.

One such underground facility was the National Institute of Microbes in Pune.

Kaanada sat exhausted in this sub-terrain research facility. It had been four weeks since the earthquake that had destroyed the structures of this Institute which stood above the ground. Most of the destroyed part had been completely demolished, and the debris almost cleared.

Kaanada had a very keen interest in sciences as a boy. He fondly remembered how his mother used to teach him about the 'world of the small.' She had repeatedly directed his learning to the tiny objects that could not be seen by the naked eye. When he used to look at microbes and their similarities under the microscope, she used to tell him to look for differences in these life forms that appeared seemingly identical. When he was old enough to understand, she also started teaching him about how the tiny units of life had their own memory and were programmed to replicate and create larger and far more complex organisms that were termed as living organisms. She also repeatedly told him how the memory of millions of organisms was coded in these seemingly tiny units and was passed over from one generation to the next. She likened this memory to the '*Akashik* records' of the 'world of the small.'

His interest took him deeper into the 'world of the small' when he started learning that various forms of life on Earth had started changing with the manipulation of the DNA by viruses. This eventually became a subject of his doctoral thesis.

Even though he was fascinated by all microorganisms, his fascination for the virus had brought him to this premier institute. He started off as an intern and now thirty years later, he was the Director heading this institute.

Most of his working life had now been spent in this underground lab. The only time he was outside was when he had to give guest-lectures or present research papers.

He even preferred to sleep in this lab and would visit his home only occasionally to meet his old mother who now lived with him in this institute campus. Even at this age, his mother had a very sharp mind and could spend hours talking with him on various microbes.

He loved the traditional food his mother cooked and made it a point to visit her during either the lunch or dinner time. The only complaint he had about her was that she would suddenly decide and travel for weeks to meet either her relatives or to visit one of the many holy places across the country.

Once, when he was chairing an international conference on viruses, he thought he saw his mother near the exit of the auditorium, wearing her typical traditional sari which had bright colours. By the time he adjusted his eyes, there was no one there. He knew that she was staying with her sister at that time and was in a different city.

He sat scratching his white hair which was barely distinguishable from his white lab coat. His eyes kept staring blankly – an expression many could not interpret if it was due to his constantly remaining behind the microscope or if it was owing to his being in deep thought.

He was now having a rapid recollection of the events in the past four weeks. The earthquake had caused only negligible damage in the underground lab. Some glass equipment had been broken. The structures that stood above the ground were completely razed to the ground. The sad part was that his team was depleted with 20 people dead.

He recalled the call from Chanakya and the Central Disaster Management team a day after the quake. Samples would be delivered daily by Chanakya's birds from across the country for testing of any virus outbreaks as per the normal Disaster Management Procedures. The number of samples arriving each day kept climbing, and there had been no respite for all surviving members of the institute who worked round the clock checking every sample that was delivered to them.

Today, he was trying to comprehend what the results of a sample that Chanakya's birds had got from the newly formed northern ridge meant.

It was a very strange prehistoric virus discovery in the sense that it was unique to all known viruses. It had managed to survive the clashing of the tectonic plates for 35 million years or possibly lay frozen and dormant in the freezing cold of the Himalayas and could now survive in the extremely hot conditions in the newly formed ridge.

He knew that these were the kind of organisms that had shaped the fate of life on earth much more than the great kings or any of the barbarian generals. For a moment, he was angry that these microbes had not got their due respect in recorded history.

By the evening, he started hearing of strange deaths across the northern edge of the country. The patterns were similar. People vomited blood and collapsed dead in less than five minutes. He knew immediately that this virus was in a hurry to replicate quickly after finding a suitable environment. It also seemed to attack multiple organs after making replicas of itself by attaching to the host DNA. Once it had attacked multiple organs, it would cause the damage and this would lead to haemorrhage, which manifested as blood being vomited by the people just before dying.

He sent word to Chanakya to ensure that these bodies are quarantined and requested for samples from these bodies.

In the next few days, he was able to connect the deaths conclusively to the newly discovered virus.

The virus epidemic was spreading so rapidly that within two weeks of the first deaths there were cases being reported not only from all over the country but even from outside. Dead bodies were piling up and mass cremations had to be restarted. Most survivors had become paranoid about getting infected and were not going anywhere near the dead. The dead bodies were now being removed by machines for cremation. The death toll had started growing so rapidly now that the number of deaths from the massive earthquake six weeks earlier had started looking smaller. On hearing about these substantial deaths Kaanada could think of only one name for this Virus – *Antyesti*.

Antyesti referred to the funeral rites performed for a dead body and literally meant 'Last Sacrifice'. The name was derived from two words *Antya* and *Isti*. The soul is said to sacrifice or return or cast off the body back to the five earth elements as it proceeds to its new destination which is determined by its *Karma* or actions. In this case, this Virus was facilitating this 'Last Sacrifice'.

Chanakya's call broke his thoughts. As he saw the 3D image of Chanakya emerge, another commanding voice could be heard. Ashoka didn't waste any words. He wanted an antivirus developed immediately. Loss of life should be stopped right away. As he spoke rapidly, Ashoka asked one very pertinent question, "What was the reason only some were dying whereas Acharya had conveyed to him that most of the Gurukul students were unaffected by the virus? What was the reason for their resistance to this virus?"

Kaanada did not have an answer.

Ever since Kaanada had laid his eyes on this virus, he had wondered what could be the possible antidote for this virus. He knew that this prehistoric virus had been eliminated in the past except maybe for a few which had been dormant or somehow survived till now and had now started multiplying. The antidote had to be simple but somehow all lab tests conducted with known anti-virus compounds tested were ineffective for eliminating *Antyesti*. Across the globe, all forums were screaming for a cure before this nemesis wiped out the entire human population.

He kept pondering on this question as he was having the *sambhar* and rice his mother had prepared in the makeshift tent that they called home now. It was strange that in this week, it was the third consecutive day that his mother had prepared *sambhar* and rice. However, he just ignored it as he had more pressing issues to resolve. Suddenly, a thought flashed across his mind – his old mother was unaffected by this virus and so were many of his older relatives. There had to be something that was common to those not affected by this virus.

He smelt the sweet aroma of the *sambhar* as it entered his mouth. Suddenly, words blurted out of his mouth along with some food he was trying to gulp. He had just asked his mother for all the ingredients of this *sambhar* to be given immediately along with the *sambhar* she had prepared.

Sambhar is a mixture of boiled *dals* or lentils, vegetables, various spices, oil or ghee mixed with a broth of tamarind pulp. It is a very common dish used all across India to be had with rice or with some Indian snacks. Kaanada's mother was originally from Tanjavoor in Tamil Nadu. She had repeatedly told him a story of the origin of *sambhar* in the kitchen of Shahuji, the Maratha ruler in Tanjavoor during the 17th century CE. Shahuji, who was a great cook himself, was trying to make a dish called *Aamti* a Maharashtrian dish. He experimented with locally available pigeon peas instead of moong beans and used tamarind pulp instead of the *kokum* used in *Aamti*. The court named this dish *Sambhar* - that is an *Aahar* or food made in honour of Sambha or Sambhaji, the second emperor of the Maratha Empire who had happened to be their guest at that time.

As he was rushing out of the tent with the *sambhar* and its ingredients his mother had just given him, he noticed from the corner of his eye that she was smiling.

Chandra had named her son as Kaanada in memory of a great teacher of the past who had founded the Vaisheshika School of Philosophy around 550 BCE where he taught his ideas about the atom and the nature of the universe. This historical teacher had authored a book 'Vaisheshik Darshan' and Kaanada came to be regarded as 'The Father of Atomic Theory'. The word Kaanada literally meant 'a teacher of small particles'.

Chandra would have loved her son to become one of the *Upagrahas*. She had taught him to understand the intricacies of the world of small and invisible when he was young and had guided him patiently in that direction. However, he was a person who preferred to be in the isolated room while being fully devoted to his work. She had taken it in her stride as a mother and as a *Nava Graha*. She was bound by the ancient rules which also clearly set out the nature of the person who could potentially be a *Nava Graha* in addition to the knowledge the person possessed.

As Kaanada rushed into the lab, he shouted instructions to test the *sambhar* as an antivirus. Within a few minutes, the tests were positive. The next step was to quickly find which of the ingredients were responsible for eliminating *Antyesti*. Once the tests were completed, tamarind proved to be the saviour. He quickly conveyed this to Ashoka who in turn had this message transmitted across the world.

Tamarind or *Tamarindus Indica* or *Imli* as it is called locally is used extensively in food preparations across the country for the taste it imparts to the food. It is also known to have medical properties and was traditionally used in *Ayurvedic* medicinal preparations. It is rich in oils, proteins, vitamins and minerals, and contains more than 50% polysaccharides. The tests had started immediately for identifying the anti-virus part of tamarind. By the end of the day, it was confirmed that vitamin C had provided protection to millions of others who had remained unaffected by the virus *Antyesti*.

All citizens were directed to have vitamin C or vitamin C rich foods till *Antyesti* was eliminated.

When the last count of the dead was confirmed, it was conveyed to Ashoka that only 30% of the population had survived. The primary task of every surviving human was to make sure that the corpses were disposed of through cremation. Everyone took the responsibility of ensuring that cremations took place quickly, and they took turns to ensure that 24-hour coverage was available to complete this task.

Ashoka found it ironic that everyone who survived had become a *Chandaal*. A person whose profession is to dispose of dead bodies is known as a *Chandaal*.

The effect of *Antyesti* was much worse in all other parts of the Earth and the human casualties were even higher in many countries. The Earth had seen five known large and sudden mass near-extinctions of various species in the past. However, this probably was the first mass near-extinction of a single species which considered itself the most intelligent on this planet.

It was confirmed later that the *Antyesti* virus had spread to the domestic animals and birds before had been transmitted to the human beings. However, it had not caused any harm to the animals or the birds that had transmitted this virus to the humans.

Punarnirmaan

P*unarnirmaan* or Reconstruction was a mammoth task. It was not just the physical aspects of people which needed restoration. It was also the way people of this country lived in relation to nature which needed to be changed.

The physical destruction of manmade things meant that people had been given a new slate to work with. It would take eighteen years for clearing all the physical memories of the past. Some of these were even reclaimed by nature in the meanwhile.

Some people preferred to live in over-ground structures while others preferred underground residences. There were those who chose a combination of above ground and below ground structures to stay. Vishwakarma and the students of *Gurukuls* had helped in the reconstruction of new structures. They were now made in stone and each of these would be in total synchronisation with their surroundings. They would never ever create the structures which would be aberrations to the eye. The reestablishment of the cities was taking longer hence most people had moved to villages and towns.

Despite the reduced population, it was decided that each public role could be taken up by a person only once for a three-year term. They were, however, free to take up another role. *Bhaarata* had truly become a nation of the people who had taken charge of the nation and were fully involved in fulfilling their duties.

There was only a single-tier representation of people. The earlier three-tier representation at the local, state and federal level was now done away with.

Additionally, all the twenty-four spokes of this democratic set up which ensured representation of people from all aspects of the nation had started shaping up as desired (See *Appendix*).

Ashoka was gradually retreating while ensuring that all people take more responsibility. He was designated as *Priyadarshi* which translated to 'A guide loved by all.'

Nine large rivers moved southwards and finally formed a *Maha Sangam* or mega union and joined at the newly exposed land which had resurfaced in the south at Kumari Kandam. This was considered as one of the holiest parts of this country and would be accessible throughout the year to the seers and sages of this country. It would also be the winter retreat of some of these great and wise people.

Kumbha Mela would now take place at this fifth location during which all other people would visit this place.

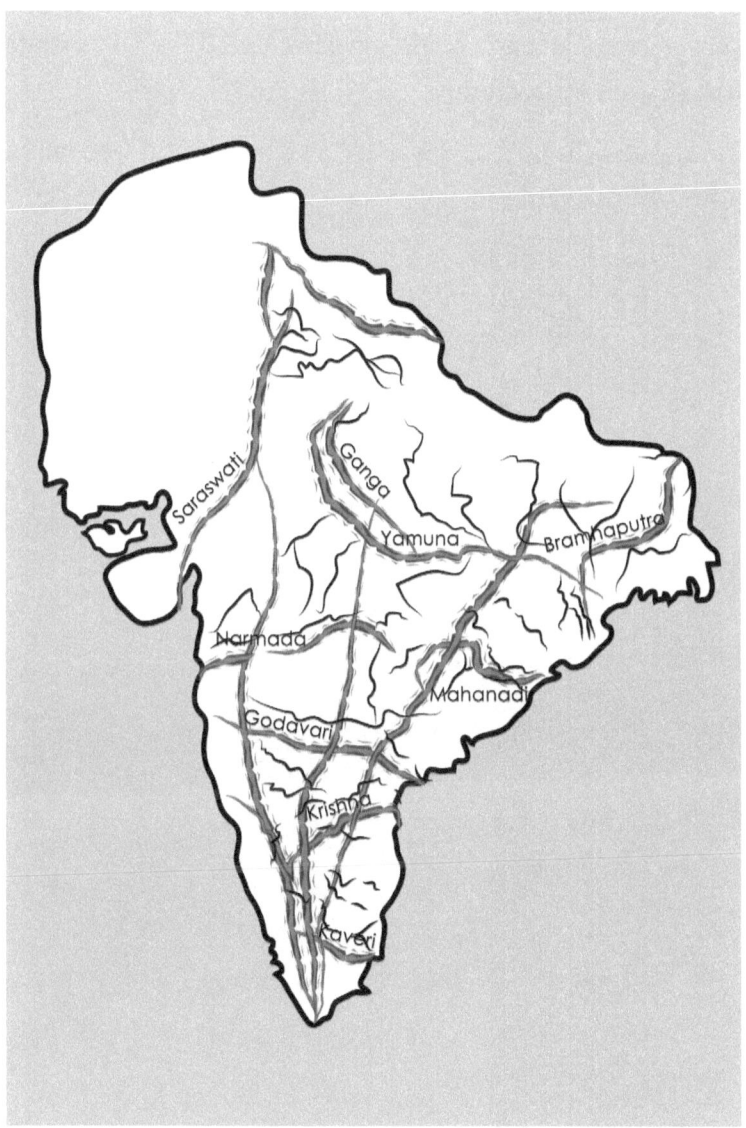

One day, as Ashoka reflected on the events of this life, he wondered if this was the preparation expected to welcome the new *Satya Yuga* or Age of Truth. He was not sure if even Gurudev could have predicted the way events had shaped up until now.

He now longed to go back to Chunar and become a potter once again.

Sampoorna Bhaarata

Post the *Antyesti* virus outbreak, all the countries surrounding *Bhaarata* had lost most of their population.

Pakistan was inhabitable due to the nuclear material scattered all over its territory. Post the massive earthquake, shoals and swarms of Chanakya's drones had been employed in the task of scavenging the nuclear isotopes scattered all over Pakistan. This was a mammoth task and would probably take a long time. Additionally, the river Indus had been merged into the newly formed river Saraswati.

On one side, there was a Golden Age which was fully established across *Bhaarata* and on the other, there was a chaotic situation in all other surrounding countries. Various groups of surviving people were trying to gain control over territories and rule of law was over. All these places were now in a constant state of civil war and anarchy. Even three years after the virus epidemic, there seemed to be no sign of peace in these neighbouring countries.

In such a hopeless state, the smaller tribes who were staying in places adjoining *Bhaarata* felt the need to be part of a peaceful and prosperous neighbour.

Ashoka and all the people voted to agree that these areas could be a part of this country. There were a few preconditions to be fulfilled. All the people living across these lands would first be identified and would have to vote in favour of this change. *Gurukuls* would then be set up across these places. Additionally, the laws of the land and the systems pertinent across *Bhaarata* would be applicable in these new regions. A slow and gradual process would ensure that this was taken care of. Once the effect of these changes was visible only then, would any of these lands be an integral part of the country.

All other areas of this newly formed island also wanted to be a part of this country. Even the widely scattered surviving tribes of far-off Afghanistan in the West remembered that they were the Gandhar region of this ancient civilisation and wanted to join this great nation.

By the end of 2070, all lands of this large island were part of *Bhaarata*. All the other islands geographically near this large island were also part of this magnificent country.

Sampoorna means whole or total. Ashoka was amazed that this was surely not exactly the *Sampoorna Bhaarata* imagined by the establishers of the great Mauryan Dynasty in the past. In fact, it was much more. It was *Sampoorna Bhaarata* that was truly total not just with respect to its geographic coverage. Even the nature and awareness of its people were *Sampoorna*. Ashoka couldn't have asked for more.

It was in the year 2076 that the people finally agreed to let Ashoka go back to his ancestral profession of pottery.

Epilogue

Ashoka reached Chunar in the evening. It was a great homecoming after almost a lifetime. He had a saffron shoulder cloth bag which contained his extra pair of clothes. The entire town had gathered to welcome their boy, who had architected the new *Bhaarata*. The celebrations started with chants of *mantras* and *aarati* and continued with songs, drama, fun and frolic and finally ended with a feast.

Next morning, he got up as usual at 5 am and had a bath in the river Ganga near his ancestral home. Back at home, his eye fell on his father's pottery wheel.

He prayed to this wheel and watered a plant next to the wheel and started slowly turning the wheel to make a pot.

As he was about to finish the pot, he saw the plant which he had watered earlier from the corner of his eyes. It had wilted and turned black. He knew from the stories he had heard at *Padma Dham* that the time had come for his solitude.

He immediately called for a *Vimana*.

He always liked watching the golden colour of the *Vimana*, he thought as he saw it land near him. Ashoka slid into the capsule which was enough for him to lie down comfortably. He looked at the control screen above him. The hydrogen fuel and the oxygen tanks were full. It was more out of habit that he saw the fuel position. He knew that the fuel would be replenished from the air as the *Vimana* travelled. He also remembered that the solar power would act as a secondary energy source. Moreover, the backup nuclear reactor pod could power this flight for another 200 solar years. He set the coordinates, and the *Vimana* started humming and then it moved towards his destination.

He got down at the east entrance of *Padma Dham* and directed the *Vimana* back to its origin.

As he approached the banyan tree, a known deep-throated voice called out, "So, you have finally come. I thought you would come sooner. Your time has come and so has mine".

Ashoka bowed down to Gurudev and said nothing.

Gurudev guided him to an inner cell behind the waterfall in the North which was totally unfamiliar to him. At the centre of this small chamber was a platform at about a foot's height. He was not sure if the ceiling was so high that it wasn't visible or was it the lack of light that was playing tricks on his eyes. He prostrated before Gurudev who blessed him before turning to close this chamber.

Ashoka sat on the platform in *Padmasana* and started his meditation with the *Omkar*.

He was not sure how long he was in meditation when suddenly he started to experience a strange feeling. It was as though he was filled with immense energy. Ashoka slowly tried to open his eyes but was unable to. He started experiencing something he had not expected.

He could observe the Crystal Cave around him. To his left, he could witness eight luminous bodies. They seemed to bow their radiant heads to him as if to welcome him to be a part of 'The Nine'. He knew that he had also now become one of 'The Nine'.

The energy he could experience was immense. It is described in the scriptures as comparable to the energy of a million Suns. It was surely not an exaggeration.

The veil of *Maya* or Ignorance which was used to create different experiences of various senses had been lifted and discarded by the infinite once again. He realised that he had remerged with the infinite and was now a No-One.

Someone had once said that "The whole was greater than the sum of its parts". He now knew how myopic the view of that person was as there was absolutely no difference between the individual and the infinite – They were One and the Same.

Being one of 'The Nine' meant that he still had some unfinished work and will have to guide humans for some time. This also meant that he had the potential to use the veil of *Maya* at will. This gave him the ability to experience the world through the senses of the humans!

He started realising one mystery after the other as he unravelled the very strange ways in which the infinite had used parts of itself to create new experiences.

He watched in awe as he explored across space and time. He could move instantly anywhere, even across great distances unheard-of by humans. He could move back into time, forward into time or even stop at a particular point in time.

As he was exploring the known universe of matter, energy and time, he suddenly felt that the universe was getting smaller. Or, was it that he was getting bigger? He was not sure and it didn't matter as everything was relative. Then the familiar universe was suddenly a small bubble from which there were multiple links to other similar infinite bubbles, which he recognised as other universes.

He could explore the other dimensions that humans had not heard of or would probably never be able to comprehend.

He moved forward in time and started observing the events that were to unfold with the change of the *yugas*.

He then got back to the present earth time. He transmitted a thought directed straight at Acharya. He followed this thought as it took the shortest possible distance and reached Acharya instantaneously. He observed how the thought wave was very different from the light wave or any other wave known to humans. As this thought entered Acharya's brain, he saw the different neurons of his brain suddenly brighten up. This thought had triggered a new set of actions originating from Acharya.

Next, he transmitted another thought. This thought wave replicated into nine similar thought waves and went in search of brains that were ready to receive them on Earth. He watched as these nine thoughts entered nine different brains. However, only one brain out of these nine had started acting on receiving these thoughts. He observed this process again and again to know the reason. All brains had the same quest at the same point in time and were therefore, able to attract the thought. However, the intensity to act on the thought was observable only in one brain in this case, and that instantaneously set a chain reaction in the neurons there.

There were lots of thoughts to be transmitted now, and he had very little time. He had to act fast and now. It was then he realised that he didn't have to.

He then started observing the thoughts moving from all 'The Nine'.

Appendix

All the twenty-four spokes of this democratic set up which ensured representation of people from a multitude of aspects of the nation had shaped up as desired by the people.

All public representatives now had a fixed and single term of three years. This applied to all the people employed for any public function as well.

However, anyone was free to represent or be employed in a different function of public life if they were allowed by the majority of the people who took the decision.

This meant that the twenty-four aspects of life enabled a smooth movement of this democratic setup.

The way these twenty-four different aspects of life shaped up is as follows:

1. Respect For All Beings And Nature

One of the basic laws of the country was the respect for all of the nature. Abuse of nature in the previous three centuries had proven how it adversely affected humanity and all life on earth. Exploitation of nature and its diversity had to be prevented at all costs. Nature had a lot to offer in terms of learning especially due to the fact that it had evolved over a longer timeframe of billions of years. Understanding and unravelling some of these secrets would help preserve humanity and other forms of life. This formed the basis of how people lived in harmony with nature.

Seas and oceans had a wealth of knowledge hidden within their depths. This knowledge was now within the reach with the technologies available. This frontier was now being explored to understand and improve human perspective. For example, life forms which exist at the depths could survive under the extreme pressures exerted by even 11000 meters of water above it or even withstand high temperatures or the extremely harsh chemical compositions there. They have no access to solar energy as the sunlight never reaches these life forms. Yet, some of this life can live a life of millions of solar years that they can be considered immortal. This was now one of the new frontiers which humans had to understand.

2. Land

There were a number of people who had acquired large tracts of land by some unlawful means or other. Very soon, the nation reclaimed most of this land. The law of this land forced those who resisted. The representatives and the people had decided that all the land would be the collective property of the nation and would never be sold. It would be shared with any of the citizens for a small annual payment. Eventually, even those people or entities that had acquired land lawfully and owned small or even large parcels of land decided to sell the land back to the nation. Thus, most of the land now belonged to the nation. Land was now no longer a commodity that could be sold or purchased, but it was the asset of the people.

3. Water

Ocean, Seas, Rivers, Lakes & Ponds, Aquifers and all other water bodies formed the sources of water. Water is the nectar which has been responsible for life to happen and flourish on Earth. It is one of the most essential needs for survival of almost all living beings.

The glacial melting in the Himalayas brought fertility to the soils of the plains. This nation had survived for a long time on the rains for filling up the reservoirs of all regions. Bad management sans a holistic approach led to uneven distribution of water with droughts in some areas or excess water in others causing floods.

Availability and understanding of various technologies which used freely available natural resources coupled with an abundant supply of free energy meant that every inch of land could be drenched with water. People had now ensured that even the arid regions had abundant water from more than one source available every moment, not just for humans but for all life forms. Care was given to ensure that all the sources of water were replenished. All the water once used would be treated for contaminants at the source of usage in micro treatment plants to ensure that it is fit for consumption by human or other life forms. This water then passed through channels meant for them. Water would no longer flow downstream only. Energy would be used to transport it upstream as well.

4. Food Providers

The food providers were the most valuable part of the society. By ensuring abundant water and natural as well as innovative natural ways of growing food devoid of manmade chemicals, this class was always able to make sure that food was available in surplus.

Some excess food would be processed or kept for later use. Much of this excess and processed food was sold to other areas within the country or sold at reasonable prices to other countries that needed it badly.

Additionally, herbs, fruits, roots, nuts, plants and trees were grown all over the country. This ensured that not only humans but animals and birds also had an abundant supply of nutrition food freely available. The survival of all life forms on earth along with humanity was never at risk from lack of food.

People had a major scare post the *Antyesti* Virus, and this had led to a majority of people preferring to eat plant-based food and not eating animals as food.

5. Textiles And Other Wearable Items

Nature has given us many resources for producing wearable items. In addition, by learning from nature, people were now able to create more and more wearable items which suited the climate and met their needs. The days of factory created artificial polymeric materials were now over. People could use 3D printers to print dresses in addition to all wearable items to suit their needs at any time by using easily available natural resources.

6. Craftsmen

People were encouraged to use handmade items. This ensured that many of the traditional arts were kept alive while innovative ones took birth.

This also gave some people an opportunity for maintaining their livelihood.

Innovative ways of using locally available natural resources also were encouraged. People were now conscious not to abuse the resources by overuse.

7. Health Of Humans And Other Life Forms

Understanding of physiology had drastically improved with the advances of nano, pico and femto sciences. All living beings were understood by their DNA make up, the movement of energies through the body and how they interacted with their environments.

Ayurveda, along with other traditional holistic natural healing methods, were now advancing and keeping pace with modern medicine. Even modern medicine was now moving towards a holistic approach in treating ailments. In many cases, they appeared to converge.

The aim of health staff was to make sure that people and the other life forms were kept fit and healthy not only by the type of liquids and food they consumed but also by the lifestyle they maintained.

8. Energy

Nature has provided us with an abundant supply of energy. This includes the Solar, Wind, Hydro, Geothermal and Tidal energies. It was ensured that the technological know-how about the best use of easily available local materials was passed on to all people. People could tap these resources and meet their energy requirements. This also ensured that the people developed creative ways to tap these resources.

One such example was learning how various chlorophyll based life forms had an ability to use solar energy and convert it into an energy type that met their requirements.

Every energy source of the electromagnetic spectrum was better understood now. This meant that the ability to convert these freely available sources into usable energy forms with greater efficiency was also better understood by people.

Additionally, the way stars light up by fusion reactions was clearly understood. This along with innovative materials and other advancements in technologies meant that safe micro-fusion reactors which replicated the fusion reactions of stars could be easily built. This technology was so advanced now that these fusion reactors could be switched on and off at the press of a button. When natural sources of energy were not available, fusion energy was available as a backup energy source.

And also, there was always an excess of energy that could be easily stored and/or distributed freely.

9. Teaching

Teaching is a very noble profession. It ensures the shaping of the future of a land. In addition to having the right knowledge and wisdom, it requires immense dedication in ensuring that this happens. The *Gurukuls* and *Vishwa Vidyalayas* ensured that the right education was imparted.

Nature now had become the greatest teacher. All kids were encouraged at a very young age to learn from this great encyclopaedia available freely all around us.

Moreover, the kids were encouraged to question and develop a deeper understanding. Hence one of the earliest lessons ensured that the fresh minds develop the ability to question. Different methods to question were taught to develop any understanding. However, the age old wisdom was not questioned. All sciences, old and new, were taught while also questioning their authenticity. *Pramanas* or proofs formed the basis of answering these questions. As the questions would grow, so would the proofs.

The limitations or boundaries of any science or its aspects would be drawn by its inability to stand the scrutiny of questioning. This ensured that the scope of this science would be clearly defined.

10. Security

Security included External Defence, Internal Law and Order, Intelligence as well as Weapons Manufacture.

It was mandatory for every citizen to be a part of security establishments when they attained the age of 21. This was a three-year training which ensured that law and order was maintained by citizens who were at their peak of physical fitness.

Anyone who wanted to be a citizen of this country had to undergo this mandatory training.

Border areas that had seen the most casualties to human life in the earlier 100 years were now entirely manned by Chanakya's robotic birds, insects and crawlers. They were equipped with various new weapons which included Vishwakarma's Intensity Rays and an assortment of forms of sounds. They would be on 24-hour and 365-day vigilance and could not be tracked by any known technology while sending instant updates to far off control centres. These weapons could inflict damage immediately based on the threat perception they would sense. It was, thus ensured that there would be no loss to any innocent soldier's lives.

Similarly, they would regularly man the waters and air. In waters, there were robotic replicas of shoals of fish and other sea creatures which took this role.

Swarms of these drones were available on standby with a very wide variety of capabilities to counter any kind of threat from any of the military forces across the globe. This meant that they were an anti-missile force that could also counter any known military weapon.

In short, they were the eyes, ears and all other senses of the security establishment. In addition to being the weapons delivery mechanism, these drones were also the weapons by themselves.

11. External Affairs

This land historically had a great relationship with all fellow humans across the globe. Hence, in the past, when people were forced to move out of their lands, this land had taken them in its fold and helped them nurture their own cultures in this country. These people continue to live harmoniously to this date. This relationship with other foreign countries and lands is said to have reached its peak under the Mauryan Empire.

A similar peak in excellent relations was now established in the present. Just like in the past, it had to be unfortunately done by sitting on a massive mountain of strength.

The experiences of the previous millennium had educated the people of this land. There were many groups of people who came to this land during this era. Many of these people had nefarious intentions and this had proven disastrous for the people of this land.

Anyone with the intention of relocating to this land was free to do so. They were also free to continue to practice their earlier customs or adapt the culture and traditions of this new place they would now call home. However, they would have to understand and respect its culture and its traditions. This was in addition to following its laws. If any of Chanakya's birds or other surveillance teams discover otherwise, they would be swiftly and dispassionately dealt with according to the laws of this land.

12. Art, Culture, Mythology and Entertainment

History has always shown that when people have all their basic needs met and peace prevails, all forms of art and entertainment start flourishing. It was no different now.

People were pursuing various forms of arts along with enjoying various forms of entertainment on a daily basis now. People would end every day with a couple of hours spent enjoying various art forms or performing them.

Mythology and history continued to be great sources of inspirational stories along with various stories which had lessons to learn from. These were also used in arts and entertainment as means of educating the younger kids.

This was a social activity which people loved to enjoy in a group and not individually.

13. Sports and Physical activities

Sports and physical activities induce a competitive spirit, and they are a means to master skills in addition to testing one's physical and mental endurance.

Keeping this in mind, kids were always encouraged to indulge in sports and other physical activities. They were also engaged in these activities for three hours every evening.

Even older people found that this stress buster had a cathartic effect and would use this time in the evenings for activities suitable for their physical ability.

This formed the basis of developing a competitive spirit, in addition to team bonding.

14. Ancient Sciences, Modern Sciences, Communication

Part of the knowledge from the ancient sciences was either corrupted or missing. Additionally, some of these had not kept pace with the other modern understandings and learning.

Once these drawbacks were removed, ancient sciences started showing modern sciences holistic ways of dealing with various day to day requirements.

On the other hand, much of the solutions offered by modern sciences did not go beyond the immediate problems. They provided quick fixes in many cases with intentions of large monetary profiteering. This had often led to various new problems being created.

Once the ancient sciences overcame their drawbacks, the modern sciences were forced to move to a holistic approach. Eventually, many ancient and modern sciences started merging while ensuring that advantages of both of these are available and drawbacks are removed.

Previous communication methods had shown how each of these could be used to influence and manipulate people. Chanakya and Vishwakarma had changed this entirely. Communication taking place across distant places had separate and dedicated networks that did not have the drawbacks of the past technologies. This was the new norm of communication.

15. Transportation and its Infrastructure

All modes of transport had a greater ability now. This could be achieved due to the free availability of energy and the great learning received from nature. Even the toughest barriers of the past were now being overcome just as in all other fields.

The new frontier that had to be explored was the greater understanding of gravity. This would eventually lead to anti-gravity transportation which would revolutionise the way humans moved from one place to another.

Humans had now come a long way from the days of the wheel. They had even shed all the past ways which had caused great harm to nature.

16. Builders, Designers and Planners

Once the massive earthquake had destroyed all the human-built structures, natural ways of building and construction were in vogue. This meant that massive aberrations to the eye and those past structures that were not in sync with nature were nowhere to be seen. This formed the new basis of any human construction activity.

Vishwakarma and Chanakya had shown how necessary structures could be created using only natural and freely available resources. This was enhanced further with innovations by the *Vishwa Vidyalayas.*

People now constructed all structures using these methods. This included even the bridges, in addition to the buildings. Inspired by knowledge gained from nature, the strongest possible fibres along with very flexible materials were used to build the best of bridges.

In addition to building durable structures that would be made using locally available materials, people also used the naturally available hills and mountains to construct places to protect them from the forces of nature.

Farmers had an issue with unseasonal rains destroying their crops. Protections to these farms from rains were made using transparent coverings that could negate this drawback.

Each such innovation meant newer and more novel ways of utilising the natural resources while remaining in harmony with nature.

17. Manufacturing

Manufacturing had drastically changed from the excesses of the last three centuries. It had become more localised to a large extent and nature was used more not only to learn, but also to produce some of the requirements. Hence, every inch of the country was mapped for the availability of every kind of naturally available resources.

The manufacturer had to pay the government for the resources used. Additionally, the wastes created from the earlier excesses were available as raw material which could be freely used as long as they did not harm nature.

One example of such manufacturing was how a wide variety of domestic animals, birds, worms and microbes were employed to generate fertilisers. These natural fertilisers would be then used along with the wastes generated from the plants to create rich and effective natural manure.

Each geographical area had small multiple factories like this to ensure that the needs of that area were met. The know-how would be passed on to all who wanted to replicate the same.

Fossil fuels had become a thing of the past. Even the products of petroleum like most polymers and chemicals were now no longer in use. If some polymers or chemicals were to be manufactured, they were to be manufactured in micro-scale and done so locally with a thorough understanding of how it would impact the nature. Enough precautions were taken to prevent any harm to nature by the manufacturing process or its products.

18. Traders and Other Service Providers

Newer services would be offered with every innovation that seemed to have grown exponentially. This also meant that most people were becoming multi-skilled.

Each service provider would use creative ways of providing their services locally.

Every person now had a quiver of skills with which they could serve the society.

This also meant that there were fewer and fewer people available for trading. Hence, most of the people preferred to make deals related to their products or services directly with their consumers. A network of all people set for this purpose met this need.

19. Financial Matters

The Currency has been a means of exchange for a very long time in history when people started trading goods and services. Money has taken various forms and every time deceitful people have found ways of cheating people.

There is yet a form of currency to be used which is devoid of all the drawbacks of all earlier forms of currency.

With this background in mind, people decided to trade goods or services for precious metals or gems or for things or services they would want. This age-old practice of exchange was restarted in addition to the existing form of currency and monetary instruments.

When goods were sold to a country outside, they would offer goods that were not locally available if they didn't have precious metals or gems with them.

The exchange value would be decided by the people making the deal.

Hoarding of any form would not be tolerated. Lesser greed meant lesser need and this translated into fair deals. Middlemen were not involved in most deals. Deals would be struck with people directly in most cases at mutually acceptable exchange rates.

The use of land and the natural resources for any commercial activity would attract a fee. This money would be used to employ various people in different government roles.

20. Election Monitoring and Control

Elections and voting had a new meaning now that people were involved in the decision-making in all aspects of the country.

A new network dedicated to voting was now available. This, like other networks, would not be connected to any other network. People could go and vote from a device at the nearest point or use specific mobile devices which were securely connected to this network. All these devices could recognise the voters by a combination of recognition techniques.

Any advice they would require on any of the aspects of a decision that was not clearly understood by them would be given by experts in that subject matter. This advice had to be objective with all the pros and cons involved. This ensured that the voter would not be influenced in any manner.

People would now never hand over this responsibility to anyone.

An important aspect of exercising the right to vote was coupled with the ability to recall a candidate who had been voted to perform a certain function. This ensured that unscrupulous people or the wrong people would never be able to represent people ever again.

21. Administration

All aspects of people's daily life required a fair degree of commonality in a society. More and more people preferred community activities as compared to individual activities.

The administrators enabled this function for a term of three years. Each administrator would be voted to office by the people of an area who wanted this administrative function. The Administration was no more a privileged job like in the past.

22. Legislature

The basis of laws created had a new meaning now. Laws were to ensure that a moral code and structure was in place.

A new scale of penalties was formed for noncompliance. This scale formed the basis of penalising a wrongdoer.

A holistic approach also ensured that various penalties for noncompliance of laws were now based on the rehabilitative approach.

If any of the wrongdoing could be reversed it had to be done so with a rehabilitation period as a punishment. A corrective approach and a 'root cause analysis approach' ensured that not just the wrongdoer but the society as a whole could be corrected if need be.

However, some crimes would be unpardonable. One such law ensured the strictest penalties with the swiftest justice for those trying to attack this land. Another was for those who try to divide the unity of the country. One more crime that would not be tolerated was trying to steal the common wealth and possessions of the people.

23. Judiciary

Judiciary in the past had huge backlogs of undecided cases. Many were being forced to wait for years or even decades to get justice.

The common man felt that justice was subverted by the rich and the powerful. The poor and the marginalised found the judicial process complex. Judiciary on its part, had failed to rise up to the expectations of the common man. This was surely not what was expected out of this system by the majority of the people.

Hence, the judiciary would always have a panel of judges who would collectively decide a case.

Efficacy with speed was expected. Frivolous cases were not to burden this system, and care to that effect was taken.

Like all other public offices, the judges had a fixed term of three years with an once-in-a-lifetime opportunity to grace this public office.

24. Astronomy & Space Exploration

All extraterrestrial space with its varied bodies that we see in the sky can give humans a very humbling feeling.

The billions of years that have shaped what we now observe in the sky have created a wide variety of matter, energy and even time itself.

Every world that exists around us is a wonderland by itself. Each of these creations is an amazing masterpiece which nature has shaped. Everything we think we understand on Earth shapes up in different ways compared to these wonderlands. These very celestial objects are responsible for creation, sustenance and destruction of life.

Hence, a basic understanding of this was taught to all as part of their formal education. This would not only create a humbling experience but also a sense of awe.

This would also inspire many to learn in detail and make an attempt to recreate some of these learning that would help us here in our one and only home - The Earth.

Glossary

Aarati: Ritual in which a deity is worshipped with fire

Akashik records: These recordings are said to be a universal record of all events, thought, actions which is maintained by nature.

Amrut: Divine nectar of immortality

Arthashastra: A 2400-year-old commentary on political strategies and economic policies written by Kautilya

Ashrams: Residing places of holy people

Atma: An individual or single soul

Avatar: Manifestation of a deity in an earthly form

Bael: Aegle marmelos. A spiny Indian rutaceous tree that bears an edible thick-shelled fruit

Bhaarata: The local name for the country called India meaning 'To be in harmony with Nature'

Chaityavriksha: A holy tree. Its wood is used for making some parts of a temple's internal structures.

Chakras: Wheels. These also indicate the cyclic nature

Chandan: Sandalwood. Used in rituals for its fragrance

Darshan: Being in the physical presence of a great master

Dhanurveda: The *Upaveda* which details various means, forms and strategies of fighting

Dhanurvidya: The art of fighting

Dharma Chakra: The wheel of *Dharma.*

Dharma: The universal law or way the nature behaves

Gurukul: A place where a Guru resides and from where he imparts Knowledge and wisdom to his pupils

Kalaripayattu: An ancient martial art form. It is considered to be one of the oldest surviving forms of martial art on Earth

Kalasha: A small pot-shaped vessel

Karma Yogi: A *Yogi* who performs selfless actions

Kumbha: A pot. It is also used in reference to the constellation Aquarius

Kumhar or Kumbhar: A Potter

Mandir: Temple

Mantras: Hymns or poetry which form the condensed version of the wisdom of the Vedas

Nava Grahas: Nine celestial bodies as per ancient astrology that have their influences on life on Earth

Neem: Azadirachta Indica. All parts of this tree are of great use to humans. The leaves act as a natural pesticide, the fruit and seeds yield medicinal oil, the bark is used to make a tonic, and the twigs are used for cleaning the teeth

Nyaya: An ancient form of logic and discretion

Omkar: Believed to be the primordial sound; Chanting of Om or Aum

Padma Dham: An imaginary place in the Himalayas. *Padma* or lotus is a flower that symbolises the ultimate flowering of a human soul. *Dham* is a place where the attachments created by the body are washed off or removed

Padmasana: A sitting posture for meditation that is said to resemble the lotus flower

Pakhawaj: A barrel-shaped two-headed drum

Paramatma: The Infinite Soul

Peepal: Ficus religiosa. A sacred fig or mulberry that is categorised as a fig native to India

Prajapati: A community of potters. It is also a name used for a ruler or emperor

Pramanas: Proofs or methods to derive proofs

Pranayama: A combination or methods of breathing practices

Pujari: Priest

Sadhu: A Holy man or one who has given up all worldly ways and leads a life in the quest of its meaning.

Sadhvi: A Holy woman

Sanathana Dharma: An eternal way of life. Hinduism is a word foreigners gave to describe *Sanathana Dharma*

Shilpi: Traditional sculptors

Shruti: Scriptures of ancient wisdom to be heard from a Master and repeated after him

Smriti: Knowledge from various ancient texts to be learnt and remembered

Surbahar: A string instrument used in Hindustani classical music.

Tantra: An ancient knowledge which reveals a deep understanding of the two opposing masculine and feminine universal forces, the relationship of these two and eventually the inevitable reunion of these

Upagrahas: Satellites of a planet

Upanishad: The end part of each Veda which contains the highest wisdom and has to be learnt from a Guru

Upaveda: Practical or applied knowledge

Vaastu Vidya and *Vaastu Shastra: Vaastu* is an ancient science of Architecture. *Vidya* means knowledge. *Shastra* means discipline or sacred writings

Vimana: A vehicle for transportation by air

Vishwa Vidyalayas: Centres of higher learning or Universities

Yogasanas: Body postures inspired from nature used by a *Yogi* to discipline the body.

Yogi: A practitioner of the ancient science of *Yoga*

Yuga: An epoch or an era. One cycle of an epoch or an era of 4.32 million solar years is called as *Maha Yuga.* This epoch was divided into four parts – The *Satya Yuga* or the Age of Truth which lasts for 1,728,000 years; *Treta Yuga* in which virtues start diminishing slowly and lasts for 1,296,000 years; *Dwapara Yuga* during which diseases and discontent become rampant and lasts for 864,000 years; and *Kali Yuga* which is the present age of ignorance and lasts for 432,000 years.

About the Author

The author is a Chemical Engineer. In his corporate career spanning more than 25 years, he has also worked with some of the top global multinationals in various roles including leadership positions in Manufacturing, Sales and Marketing.

He now lives in Pune, India, with his wife Aarati, son Varad, daughter Saanika and a Beagle, Snoopy.